Drought
& Other Stories

Drought
& Other Stories

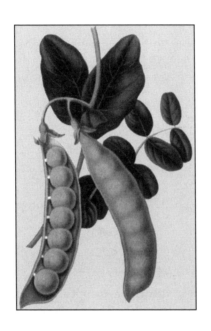

Jan Thornhill

Cormorant Books gratefully acknowledges the support
of the Canada Council for the Arts and the Ontario Arts
Council for our publishing program. We acknowledge the
financial support of the Government of Canada
through the Book Publishing Industry Development
Program (BPIDP) for our publishing activities.

THE CANADA COUNCIL | LE CONSEIL DES ARTS
FOR THE ARTS | DU CANADA
SINCE 1957 | DEPUIS 1957

Some of these stories have appeared in *This Magazine,
The Malahat Review, The Fiddlehead, Fireweed,
Room of One's Own* and *Quarry Magazine.*

Printed and bound in Canada.

Canadian Cataloguing in Publication Data
Thornhill, Jan
Drought & other stories
ISBN 1-896951-26-0
I. Title. II. Title: Drought and other stories.
PS8589.H5497D76 2000   C813'.6   C00-900673-7
PR9199.3.T482D76 2000

CORMORANT BOOKS INC.
RR 1, Dunvegan, Ontario K0C 1J0

For my mother

Contents

Drought   1

Violation   11

Not for Meat, but for Love   19

Goldfish   29

Pinned   39

Saint Francis and the Birds   53

Waiting   65

Action   77

Life in the Country   89

Simple Solutions   101

Females are Green, Stupid   113

Extremes   125

Worms in the Back Garden   133

Dirt-Eater   139

Drought

She keeps finding bones in the woods. Some have been sawed, some gnawed. All are meatless. They are old bones, green with mossy algae, slippery to the touch, painted in emerald-tinted lard. They stay buttery even on the driest days in that driest of Julys, last year's leaves crunching unnaturally underfoot when they ought, by rights, to be rotting into layered loam, black and moist and smelling rich enough to eat. In better, wetter years, she brings wheelbarrows full of that forest soil to the garden for her plants, for her beans and tomatoes and rhubarb chard. Chocolate cake of the earth, she likes to think. She feeds it to them, digs it in for dessert.

But this July the drought has affected the collective memory of those leaves; they've forgotten the art of decay. It's a double tragedy of sorts, that dearth of rain: leaves refuse to rot and mushrooms refuse to grow. Other than lichen-like turkey-tails fanning out from fallen trees, the only fungi fruits are Russulas, pretty but chalky and bland. Unedible as opposed to inedible or, as someone put it, better kicked than picked. Which she does sometimes. Kicks them. Hard. Out of frustration. So brittle they burst like snowballs upon impact with the toe of her rubber boot.

The bones. She doesn't know what creature once belonged to them, what creature's tendons, muscles, sinews once latched them one to another, rubber bands controlling the movement of limbs and joints. She knows nothing of anatomy. They could be the remains of deer, or cows. For all she knows they could be human. Two young girls from town disappeared some time ago, have never been found.

Probably, though, they are the bones of deer. This she can see as frame-by-frame possibility, a deer running frantic from a rifle crack, from the ripping, rippling (she imagines) pain of

1

a bullet wound, zigzagging between the trees, leaving in its wake some man, heart pumping, cussing aloud—how could he have missed?—the creature running and running until, far away, it collapses, last feeble beats of heart throbbing into the earth it lies upon, where, eventually, its remains are picked clean by scavengers, by foxes, coyotes. Meatless bones discarded, spread randomly throughout the woods, as if by slo-mo explosion.

Where she lives, hunting season for deer is two weeks long. Marked on her calendar in red, transferred from one year to the next, like birthdays and the first hard frost and last. Two long weeks she stays inside, venturing into neither the garden nor the woods. Keeps Jocko in as well. Hunters, she has decided—the trespassing types (the only kind that stalk through these woods that surround her house)—are idiots. As proof of this, she has a silver X of Christmas tape patched over a crizzle-edged hole in her kitchen window, tape that keeps the warmth of winter fires in, the mosquitoes of summer out, an X that reminds her—it's right in the centre of her vision when she gazes out towards the garden while her hands, submerged in lemon-scented water, feel for the last of the cutlery, dish detergent bubbles whispering in agreement—what idiots they are. How very dangerous they are.

Nothing, though, explains why some of those bones are sawed.

The first time he comes she is in the garden, hunkered over, squishing aphids, her fingerprint whorls dyed green, slippery with half-digested plant juices. Jocko explodes into his car-arrival dance. He's not a big dog, but some husky genes have given him a barrel chest and long dense fur growing from the flesh folds of his neck. His hackles, up, are impressive, threatening to the uninitiated, like the dorsal fins of sharks. His bark is stiletto sharp, ear-puncturingly so, but has a carrying power she, who lives alone, appreciates. He drives his paws into the gravel of the drive like hoofs, front legs stiff. His curled plume of a tail doesn't wag; that would give him away for the suck he really is.

She watches through the leaves to see if this stranger will have the nerve to get out of his vehicle. He's invisible because the windshield has the sun, but she knows, at least, it can't be Jehovah's Witnesses, who travel only in packs of four, in American-made sedans, two men in front, two women behind. Always, because of Jocko, it's the women who get out. That's their rule. From consultations with neighbours, she knows this to be fact. If there is a dog, the women get out. No dog, the men. But this is no sedan, it's a pickup truck, a two-tone Silverado, grey and red.

She smiles, hidden behind the tendrils, behind the soft green leaves and silky pods of sugar snap peas, when the door of the truck sweeps open. A man climbs out. A fearless man.

The pitch of the dog's bark rises an octave. She can hear, too, the animal's feet shovelling loose driveway gravel atop his claws.

"Ah, shaddap," the man says, not meanly, nor aggressively, but with the tolerance of someone who can see Jocko's show for what it is but doesn't want to hurt the dog's feelings.

She watches his hand go out, low, offering the invisible gift of scent, the dog's snout jerking forward. The hand halfway disappears into Jocko's ruff, massaging absent-mindedly. The stranger is looking not at the dog but expectantly towards the house, ruddy-faced, his floridness exaggerated by the green frame of leaves she's peering through. The dog flips neatly then, bellies up into submission and she, standing, calls out a noncommittal "Hello."

He has a fake eye.

"It's glass," he says immediately, because she is avoiding looking at it, standing there in the drive. "Lost it to a screwdriver, would you believe?" Offering no more explanation than that, she biting her tongue although she's dying for the details, and will imagine them later, after he has gone.

He stands before her in all his one-eyed glory, telling her that he has permission from Ellis, the farmer who owns the woods that surround her home, to hunt for bears. He pronounces it "beers", says, too: "Just so's you know. I'll be parked out there, off and on, like."
She finds it strange, a little, that Ellis has agreed. The property is posted No Hunting, off limits, at least to those who want to shoot deer. She shrugs, tries to stare at the bridge of the stranger's nose, but her eyes dart unintentionally to first the glass eye, then the living one. The power of each, in its own way, is exquisite. She frightens herself by inviting him in for a cup of tea.

He spills it, his tea, an action that seems premeditated in its clumsiness.
"Depth perception problems," he says.
She fusses over the spill with a rag, wondering how he drives in two dimensions, but doesn't ask.
Nonchalantly fishing, but heart rate increasing with the question, she asks if he intends to sell the gallbladders of the bears he kills. She's heard of this, five thousand dollars a pound by the time they reach the Orient, dehydrated into shiny little fists. She's seen it on the news.
He scoffs at the question with a snort. Leans towards her, whispers confidentially, "You've never really eaten meat till you've tasted *beer*."
There is history. He hunted bear in these woods before, he says, with Ellis's permission, until ten years ago, stopped two years before she moved in.
"The wife," he says, "she didn't like it." He blinks slowly, a deliberate folding of flesh atop both the glass eye and the other, normal one.
Her own eyes, looking for the wife, flit to his ring finger—naked, she sees, except for unruly, well-spaced hairs. The hand is broad, the fingers short, the nails are flat and clean. She startles herself by imagining how those fingers would feel

tracing circles around her nipples, slowly and leisurely, before lightly pinching them. Heat prickles her cheeks.

"Took a while," he says, "but I finally took care of her."

He smiles, then winks, a glass-eye wink that shocks her so deeply she nearly gasps aloud.

At his truck, he shows her a box of donuts. They are Hawaiian donuts, heavily sprinkled with multicoloured sugar pellets. Thinking he is offering her one, she reaches out. He slaps down the lid. Might as well have slapped her face.

"You don't want 'em," he says, "Day-olds. *Beers*, they got like a sweet tooth, but they don't give a good goddamn how fresh a donut is."

He's going to put them out there in the woods. Someplace moist where, tomorrow, he can look for tracks.

Tomorrow. She is waiting even before the sound of his truck is gone.

Jocko is barking at the end of the drive. She can see the Silverado's chrome glinting between the shins of the roadside trees. So he's in the woods. He hasn't stopped to say hello. Sitting in the kitchen she feels like an idiot, but nonetheless feels spurned.

Jocko's barking intensifies. Her heart flutters at the crunch of gravel. Hand tidies hair.

He's going to bait the bears.

"How?" she asks. She has been able to make herself watch his lips and tongue as he talks, but when she must speak, when his mouth is at rest, as now, that still eye is a powerful magnet. A hair is lying across it, which apparently bothers her much more than him. An eyelash.

"Meat," he says, and she is back with his lips and tongue. She is so conscious of them that she can't help but let them wander over her, from neck to breastbone to belly, while, standing on the porch, he tells her about the meat he plans to use. Unfit for human consumption. Ungradable pork, from a local butcher.

"Where?" she asks.

"I'll lay 'er out by the swamp," he says. "Below the blind."

"The blind?"

At first, it is she who leads him.

From the house into the woods she has routes, routes that differ with different species' seasons, though none are paths. Chanterelles, mid-summer, straight ahead amongst the pines; to the left, at the base of the hill, sporadically appearing king boletes, warm fawn caps umbrellaed by spruce and balsam boughs; anise-scented oysters to the right, moist white steps that ladder up standing dead poplars at the height of the mosquito and blackfly overlap, the same place that morels, two weeks earlier, pop up at the same poplars' feet. Normal years, that is.

"This way," he says, leading her beyond the grassy clearing where fragile-toothed hedgehog mushrooms grow.

Jocko is with them, has been bounding back and forth, is now hauling between his jaws a ten-foot limb he expects someone to throw for him. Discards it when he finds himself wedged, once too often, between two trees. Leaves crunch and brittle branches crack beneath their feet. Black nodules sprout from the ground.

"Dead man's fingers," she says.

"Come again?" He looks at her as if she is mad. As if it is she who might murder him, and not the other way around. She has not been conscious of either possibility before.

She wrenches from its rootlike anchor one of the growths, woody and gnarled and black. A crooked thumb.

"It's a fungus," she says. "Like a kind of mushroom. You can't eat it, though."

"Wouldn't want to," he says.

"I eat other wild mushrooms." She is aware that she has said this for shock value.

He actually stops in his tracks. Looks at her with great seri-
ousness. "Some a them are poisonous."

"I know," she says lightly, with pride.

He moves on. She is sure she hears him say, "Kill yourself
if you want."

The blind. Wedges of two-by-four nailed as steps up the
trunk of a huge old pine, rising to a small braced platform
large enough to sit upon but not to lounge on. All painted
black. She's not surprised that she has never seen the blind
before; when she walks the woods, it is face down, eyes to the
ground.

She knows the spot, of course, the needle-encrusted earth
just short of becoming spongy with swamp. A place she sel-
dom goes, where only slippery Jills and chicken-fat Suillus
grow, not her favourites—slimy as slugs when cooked, if
their soft flesh isn't already honeycombed by miniature,
wriggling worms. And yes, there are more bones here than
elsewhere, she remembers, she sees.

"Why is it called a blind?" she wants to know.

"Just is," he says.

It seems densely intimate, standing amidst the forest smells
with him. Achingly so.

He comes back at sunset, after he has dumped a sack of meat
near the base of the pine. She asks if he wants a beer.

"To drink," she clarifies unnecessarily.

They sit on the porch surrounded by the white-noise hum
of mosquitoes. Drought or no drought, there are always mosquitoes.

He is tense and unfocused, fidgets his feet, breathes
raggedly through his nose, his nostrils flaring, while they talk
in circles around nothing. She sees muscles in his neck, his
jaws, define themselves, then relax. He is contagiously elec-
tric. It enters into her through her chest, spreads warmth
between her thighs.

"Well," he says, standing. "Time to get up there and wait for *beers*." Smiling almost coyly, live eye so bright it illuminates her misunderstanding.

She lies in bed, awake, waiting to hear a shot, knowing now, somehow, that it can't possibly be bear-hunting season. It's July. Knowing that he's never spoken to Ellis. Knowing that he is perched up there, waiting in the darkness twenty feet above the forest floor, kept warm by his own anticipation that she thought was meant for her.

Three more dusks he comes, parks up the road, avoids her driveway, does not stop by. Each time, Jocko announces that he is there, barking five minutes the first night, three the second, but, by the third, offering only a couple of perfunctory, hollow woofs before returning to his night curl, tail tip keeping bloodsucking insects off his nose. Three nights she lies awake, morbid images clarifying. Three mornings she hears his truck pull away at dawn.

It is two weeks since he last was there. It is barely light. Before eating breakfast, she takes her basket, tells herself that it's chanterelles she's looking for although, still, it hasn't rained. Not a drop. Pointed tips of beech and maple leaves are curling, turning brown. Jocko she leaves at home.

She can smell the putrefaction before she reaches its source, braces herself for the sight she has been imagining at night, in bed. Big black bear lying on the ground, on its back, legs sprawled, bullet hole in head, another wound, this one gaping, in its abdomen where the gallbladder would have been. It will be seething with maggots, especially around the eyes, which will no longer be there. Raw sockets filled with larval movement.

But when she gets to the spot there is no bear, only pork, multicoloured meat rotting away from sawed bones. The smell is intense.

She stands swaying for a moment before she begins to climb. It's more difficult than she has imagined, the steps being a foot and a half apart, and her heart is thumping hard even before she hauls herself up onto the platform. The plywood is sprinkled with rust-coloured needles. Hollow remnants of tent-caterpillar cocoons cling to the rough bark where the platform abuts the tree. Arranging herself cross-legged, she has not yet had the guts to look down. She knows the height will seem exaggerated.

She is right. She is vertigiously high above the ground. So high she believes she may never be able to climb down. Blue jays are queedling, and somewhere, farther away, a crow caws. Pine boughs spread out around her, above her, below her. The smell of decomposing flesh saturates the air.

She covers her left eye with her hand, looks downwards through the other to see what he saw, to see the way he saw it. Blinding an eye like that causes the depth of the forest to disappear. Suddenly dizzy with the closeness of the ground, she takes her hand away.

Breathing lightly and quickly, forcing herself, she presses her hand to her eye again. She knows she will become used to it eventually, will become inured to the flatness, to the banality. And when that happens, she will be able to climb down. One-eyed and lacking perspective, she waits for that moment to come.

Violation

Ally found that she was becoming consumed by constant irritation. The irritant, she knew, was Jake. Not because of his indiscretions with other women, his blatant philandering, which had always been a given in their relationship, but because of his reckless nature, the close partnership he enjoyed with his adrenal glands that she did not share with her own. This, she realized, was kind of funny since it had been that part of Jake's character that attracted her to him in the first place.

Before long, Ally redefined the irritation as a form of jealousy. She felt that she herself was a coward, that she was afraid to take chances, that she lived a dangerous life only vicariously through her relationship with Jake. Her own existence took on a new insignificance because of this, as if she were a peripheral character on a TV show, a TV show that wasn't even a hit, and this saddened her.

Ally opened her door in the rooming house to two men who roughly pushed their way in, one with a sparkly gold stocking compressing his features, the other wearing a plastic Darth Vader mask. Darth carried a baseball bat. The other man bandied about a sawed-off shotgun.

"Where's the money?" Darth demanded in an un-Darth-like voice.

The money? Ally was confused. The situation instantly became dreamlike. "What money?"

"Fuck," said Stocking Face.

Ally had never felt so innocent. She wondered if she should tell them where her money was, her mayonnaise jar full of pennies. Earlier in the day she had separated the dimes and nickels from the coppers, finding only just enough silver to pay for a small pack of smokes.

"On the floor," said Darth. He pointed to the floor with his bat in case she didn't understand.

Ally lay down quickly, on her stomach. Stocking Face pressed the cold barrel of the gun against her temple. He was wearing black cowboy boots with white stitching. Darth wore grubby sneakers.

"The money," said Darth.

Were they blind? Couldn't they see where they were? Even from the cracked linoleum floor, Ally could. Stained walls, frayed furniture, mismatched mugs and plates, ashtrays and beer glasses pursed in bars. She suddenly regretted never having sprung for a mop on cheque day.

"There's no money," she said, feeling strangely calm, centred in the eye of the storm her vibrating body had become, heart pounding, saturated in adrenalin. Is this how Jake feels? she wondered.

"Fuck," Stocking Face said again. His voice sounded far away.

The shotgun was still pressed against her temple, long enough now that Ally could no longer feel the end of the barrel as a cold metal circle. It had warmed to her, was now just an even pressure, the brother of an incoming migraine. Her left ear, the one sandwiched between her skull and the floor, was beginning to throb numbly. She closed her eyes and allowed herself to kick off into the rush of her blood, glided away with it, did a slow, leisurely breaststroke, afloat on the grimy surface of the linoleum floor.

Darth was rifling her shelves and drawers. Books clunked to the floor, magazines slid across the linoleum, dishes rattled, coat hangers shrieked along the metal pole in the clothes closet. All those sounds seemed muted, as if Ally were listening to activity in a neighbouring room through the thick bottom of a glass tumbler—which, in fact, she had done on occasion.

The clatter of coins cascading to the floor brought her

sharply back to the moment. Darth had found her penny jar. She opened her eyes in time to see the queen's face rolling past her own.

"Fuck," said the man with the big vocabulary.

"Where the hell's the money, Sharon?" said Darth. He was getting pissed off.

Ally was amazed at how a single conglomeration of letters, spoken, could change the course of her life so dramatically, so significantly, so instantly.

"*Sharon* lives upstairs, you idiot," she said.

When Darth lifted his mask high enough to spit on the floor on his way out, Ally saw a fuzzy brown caterpillar crawling above his upper lip. It wasn't until he had replaced the mask that she realized the caterpillar was meant to be regarded as a moustache. Stocking Face was more violent and kicked her in the side, hard, before he left. Ally was beyond feeling, and even forgot that she had been kicked until the next day, when a beautiful purple trophy blossomed on the spot where the black toe of the scuffed cowboy boot had met her ribs.

After that event, Ally began lusting after details. She tried to extract them from Jake. Sometimes she asked politely, sometimes begged, at other times tried to coerce with woman-to-man bribes, but Jake steadfastly refused to tell her the intricacies of his B&Es and his (less frequent) armed robberies, wouldn't give her the dirt on his narrow escapes, his brushes with the law, would only gift her with hoop earrings for her unpierced ears and lines of clinical cocaine, or treat her to big meat meals and other perks paid for with the profits of his crimes. Exasperatingly, he would repeat conversations with pawnbrokers and fences verbatim, after-the-fact things, but as to how, exactly, he entered a drugstore or house, whether or not he met anyone there, whether or not he was afraid, about those critical details his lips were zippered shut. He shared with her only the sharp, sour olfactory remnants of dangerous activity. It drove her crazy. There were so many unanswered questions. Did he ever pistol-whip a clerk? Did he wear a balaclava? Gloves? Did he wipe his feet upon entering someone else's private domain? Did he sample their food? Jake was tight-lipped about those things.

"The less you know the better, sweets," he would say, and snap his gum or wink.

Jake made one mistake too many. Ally knew of this mistake possibly before he did.

Shortly after he left one afternoon, Ally's friend Nan dropped by with a six-pack; Nan was a good friend and was well aware of what times of the month Ally was low on funds. Halfway through the beer, Nan discovered in the bathroom that her period had started unexpectedly.

"Can I borrow a rag?" she called out.

"I'd rather you kept it!" Ally shouted back.

When Nan returned she was dangling something from her index finger. "Taken up a new line of work?" she asked. It was a .38. "Found it in with the maxi-pads," she said.

"What an asshole," said Ally, smiling fondly, shaking her head.

She thought it was kind of cute, in a stupid sort of way. Although he hadn't said where he was going, she knew Jake had gone out on a job. He'd had that antsy way about him and he drank almost a whole litre of orange juice in one go, standing in front of the refrigerator, tilting the cardboard container into his mouth. She'd watched his Adam's apple bob.

"Guess he forgot it," she said. "That'll be a surprise."

Later, she got a phone call from Jake. It was the only call he was allowed to make. She had to find him a lawyer. She had to post bail. When he said that about the bail, her eyes focused on her penny jar.

"Sure, Jake," she said. "Don't worry."

While Jake was away, Ally started reading the paper, the one that avidly reported crimes. She looked for small but telling details. She collected new questions to ask Jake when he got out. Did he ever make sandwiches for himself and then leave the dirty dishes in a stranger's sink? Did he ever watch TV? Had he ever shat somewhere other than in a toilet in any of his victims' homes?

Ally was startled one day by a thought: I have shared my bed with a man who may or may not have left a turd on someone's wall-to-wall carpeting.

Jake was gone so long that Ally had to start picking up strangers in bars. She carried Jake's .38 in her purse, just in case.

She wandered around the strangers' apartments whenever she was left alone and fingered their belongings. There was never anything worth stealing, although sometimes she emptied their wallets of money if she had the opportunity, but that she didn't think of as theft. She figured they owed her.

She read an article in the Sunday edition of the paper written by a reporter whose home had been broken into. The writer made it clear that she equated having her belongings touched by a phantom thief with sexual assault. Ally thought that was a bit much. She herself had been sexually assaulted in the past, and she had also had her belongings touched by Darth Vader. There was no comparison between the two. The only way she had been affected by the intrusion into her room, she was sure, was that she had become suspicious of moustachioed men and those who sported black cowboy boots with white stitching, although she was not entirely sure she had not already felt that way before the incident. Unquestionably, sexual assault was in another category.

She read the article several times, trying to understand this other woman's point of view. One line was particularly compelling: "The worst was that they moved things around in my refrigerator!" Ally found the exclamation mark riveting. It occurred to her that because the two men who had pushed their way into her room had never gotten around to looking in her refrigerator, she would never know if that particular violation of her personal space would have bothered her or not.

While a man whose apartment she was in was pouring two fat fingers of Scotch into a tumbler for her, Ally, on a whim, opened his refrigerator and looked inside. She took a quick inventory: five bottles of beer; a yellow plastic squeeze container of hot dog mustard; a half-empty jar of Miracle Whip; an unopened jar of pickled jalapeño peppers; a can of cream soda. All and all, a curious lack of food.

"What are you doing?" the man accused.

"Just looking," she said.

"Well, don't," he said, putting his hand on Ally's and helping her close the door.

Aha, she thought.

She tried it again with the next man. There was a plastic squeeze bottle of mustard in his refrigerator also. He was more forcefully upset than the first man.

"Get out of my fridge," he said, as if she had done something inexcusable, as if he were rebuking a cat who had left a hairball or mouse entrails in his shoe.

Later, in bed, he couldn't even get it up.

Ally took to carrying one of the hot Polaroid cameras that Jake could never find a market for in her bag along with the gun.

"Chuck you, Farlie," she whispered when she took pictures of the men she had fucked after they had fallen asleep, their mouths slack.

"What is this?" Jake asked in a letter. "Who the hell are these assholes you're sending me pictures of?"

Ally let a man in a seersucker suit buy her drinks and oysters Rockefeller. He was bitter that his wife had left him for a taller, less successful man. Although he seemed mild-mannered in the bar, when he got her in bed he was rough. He pinched her nipple, hard. He twisted it.

"You like that," he said, staring intently into her pained eyes.

He was on top of her and had her pinned down by her wrists, held above her head. Ally didn't struggle until he turned her over and tried to take her up the ass. His small, soft hands were surprisingly strong.

"No," she said, but he was too powerful for her.

The man apologized afterwards. He didn't look at her as he spoke; he was, instead, intent on the condom he was peeling off his flaccid penis.

"Don't worry about it," Ally said. It came out flat, without emotion, as she meant it to. Fleetingly, she thought about the gun in her bag.

She asked the man if he would mind if she spent the night. He raised his eyebrows, recoiled enough that a double chin appeared, but said sure, yeah, no problem.

Lying beside this man, Ally stared up at the ceiling and listened to the hum of his air conditioner, the drone of the city outside, the hissing of her seething nerves. She didn't mind the time it took for him to fall asleep; it only served to magnify her anger, a magnification which, at that moment, was agreeable to her. She waited until he began to snore, then slipped off the bed and dressed furtively. The flash didn't wake him. She sneaked out of the room carrying her shoes, tiptoeing like a cartoon burglar.

She opened the refrigerator door and smiled when she saw the mandatory squeeze container of mustard. She knew what she would do with that.

Ally worked quickly, quietly, efficiently, subtly altering items on the shelves. With her fingers, she removed a slippery half-moon from an open can of peaches and submerged it in a large jar of spaghetti sauce. Using a knife she found in the sink, she mined into a tub of margarine, dropped a pimento-stuffed olive in the hole, smoothed it over again. She pulled a mouldy strand of noodles from a Chinese takeout container and buried it deep in a jar of raspberry jam.

Pausing, stumped for a moment by the eggs, Ally was suddenly acutely aware that she was flying on adrenalin, fearlessly aloft, sublimely attuned to the rhythms of her body, to her surroundings.

"Aha," she whispered.

She spied a carton of orange juice in the door, unscrewed the lid of the plastic spout, cracked an egg, and, using her cupped hand as a funnel, watched first the white of the egg, then the yolk, slither down the hole. She put the eggshell evidence in her purse.

Ally was happier than she had been in she didn't know how long. She had found her calling, she was sure. Perhaps, she thought, she would cryptically thank Jake, perhaps not. Certainly, though, she would send him the picture. No details, just the picture.

After spitting in the mustard container and replacing its lid, Ally stood back from the refrigerator, aimed the camera from her hip, and pushed the red button.

"Stick 'em up," she said, before the camera spat the Polaroid into her hand.

Illuminated only by the light of the open refrigerator, Ally, poised for flight, watched the picture slowly evolve from dull blue-grey into a bright, crisp-edged image of the crime she had so blithely, so blissfully committed, a violation only she could see.

Not for Meat, but for Love

I bring him gifts to woo him. Again I am the wooer, not the wooee. I don't mind really, because I know I'm good in the role, perhaps because I'm so sure of how easily I myself could be won if someone ever took it upon himself to woo me. The first is a phoebe, a dainty flycatcher that in life bobs its tail up and down as an identifying trait, but that in death lies limp as a sodden Kleenex in my hand after I find it lying on the ground beneath my living-room picture window.

I met him at a local party.

"And how do *you* manage to make a living in this wilderness?" I asked.

I am always curious even though it's not really a wilderness, it's farmland and woods and a few cottage lakes. I've only been out here a short time and still find it interesting to know how people go about making money when there are few obvious means of doing so. So far I've met a chainsaw salesman, a maple syrup producer, a barber who raises beef cattle on the side, a couple who grow sweet corn and rutabagas to sell on the highway in the late summer, and three men who—it seems an amazing coincidence—are all carpenters working on the same nuclear power facility being built an hour and a half's drive away. It seems less amazing when one of them tells me that the project employs more than four thousand men, a high percentage of whom are carpenters hired to put up scaffolding and take it down again, over and over and over again.

I popped a potato chip in my mouth, waiting for his answer. For a moment he said nothing, it was just his eyes getting a fix on mine.

"Taxidermy," he said, finally. He took a deep breath. "I'm a taxidermist."

I did not blanch as I could tell he expected me to.

The second gift is a crow. I spot it beside the highway, shining black on the gravel of the shoulder. When I pull over, a gust of wind lifts its wing from its body in one final, solemnly flippant wave.

I am nervous. There is a distinct possibility that the crow has been dead long enough that flies have come, have laid their eggs. That the eggs have had time to hatch.

There was a squirrel in my childhood, in the ditch on the route home from school. Suzy and I rolled it over with a stick. Have you ever looked closely at whitecaps on a lake, maybe over the side of a boat? Rolling and boiling—roiling, I think, is a good word. Creamy white maggots. It was such a startling image, so unexpected, that it took a moment for us to gasp, for the stomach-turning revulsion to set in.

I do the same with the crow, but with the toe of my shoe. I roll it over. I am relieved that it's only black feathers that I see, a few grains of grey gravel clinging to them. A dribble of blood has crusted in the hinge of the bird's beak. Otherwise it is unmarked, a perfect specimen for taxidermy.

These bird corpses are not just gifts, they are a calculated excuse to appear, uninvited, at his door. He is good-looking, and since the party I've been having fantasies—in the bath, where all my best fantasizing is done. There is a scar on his cheekbone, a glazed arc of purplish skin. I imagine running my finger along its length, my tongue. I imagine never asking him how he got it.

Both times that I stand there, waiting after I knock, I feel as if I'm the reincarnation of a cat I once had, Satin, who, up until the day he died, brought me offerings of songbirds he had caught, and mice, and bats. I would find them in my shoes, on my pillow, on my doorstep. Sometimes they were not quite dead.

When I first moved up here, I had a brief thought that I would get another cat, to keep me company, but on second thought I realized that I have no interest in sharing my home with a gratuitous killer again—Satin never ate any of those creatures he caught, he simply tortured them for his own amusement. I have since seen a country cat deal with a mouse with what I imagine must be the proper finesse—a mercifully quick crunch to the skull before swallowing the animal whole, head first, tail dangling out from between the cat's lips for a moment before it disappears, sucked in like a strand of spaghetti. But I know if I were to get another cat it would be just my luck to get another one who was inept at his job, one who avoided the kill in order to savour the long moments of terror to which he repeatedly subjected his smaller, helpless victims.

I had a boyfriend like that, once, back in the city.

I had never met a taxidermist before, so at the party I pumped him for information. He told me that he prefers birds because they offer him a greater range of lifelike poses to choose from than the fish he's mostly asked to stuff. Fish are his bread and butter.

But the problem with fish, he said, is that in real life they don't do much other than swim around. They don't flirt or sing or preen. Usually the most exciting, most acrobatic moment of their lives, from a human point of view anyway, is that panicky instant they are suddenly yanked, flopping and gasping, from their own watery element into ours.

The anglers, the taxidermist told me, say things like "She put up one hell of a fight, so see if you can make her look that way...you know, make her thrash around." Others tell him they don't care how he does it, just so long as he makes the "fucker look big."

"Excuse the language," he said after that last bit, further endearing himself to me. (Men out here, I have found, are much more gallant than city men. It's an attractive quality I first noticed at the beer store, when the man behind the counter offered to carry my twelve-pack to the car.)

He confided in me: because he is fairly new at the game, he practises on roadkill. Of course, he told me, he'd like to do more mammals, but mammals are frequently damaged beyond repair by the cars and trucks that hit them, and he's not a hunter himself, so that option is out. I almost swooned when he said he doesn't hunt. I'm a vegetarian and don't believe in killing animals for food, let alone for trophies for rec-room walls.

"Birds, though," he said, "are more often just grazed by a windshield or a headlight, stunned to death. That's best."

We each had a potato chip then, a crunchy pause in our conversation.

"Don't tell anyone about this roadkill stuff, eh?" he said finally, nearly a whisper.

I felt privileged, almost caressed, to be taken like that, into his confidence.

He is delighted with my gifts, each of them. Both times he turns them in his hands, riffles their feathers, spreads their wings. There are no marks on either of them, no abrasions.

"A few lice," he says of the crow.

"Oh, I'm sorry," I say, thinking that the bird is spoiled.

"No, no," he says. "Lice are no problem. I just dust them with poison before I begin."

I'm so overwhelmed by relief that I know right away I've fallen in love with him.

Both times he invites me into his kitchen and offers me something to drink, coffee for the phoebe, beer for the crow. I'm not sure if the offer of beer the second time is progress or coincidence, but I take it as the former and proceed to tell him incredibly personal things about myself. While I talk, I shred the label off my beer bottle to keep my hands busy, to keep myself from reaching over to his face, to his scar.

He shows me his collection of eyes. They come in all different sizes and colours. The tiniest are for hummingbirds and mice, the largest for deer and owls. Great horned owl eyes are larger than wolf eyes, a bit of trivia I expect I would never otherwise have come across.

In a small wooden case he keeps a set of "special" eyes for ring-necked pheasants. They are tricoloured, as exquisite as jewels.

"I haven't had a pheasant yet," he says, "but I got the eyes anyway. I figure maybe having the eyes will help to bring me the bird." He gives me a sideways sort of smile, searching my face with his eyes, visually frisking me for what I think of what he's just said.

"That makes perfect sense," I say, to put him at ease, because I want desperately for him to be easy around me, for him to say anything that pops into his head, for him to blurt out that he's just as smitten by me as I am by him. Wistfully, I imagine him months from now, stuffing a bird into the shape of a heart to present to me on Valentine's Day.

My wooing isn't working. Although I have given him my phone number, he doesn't call. Days pass. I sit in the old farmhouse I'm renting, staring out the window at fields that have lain fallow for years. It's late summer and the goldenrod begins to blotch the hills with yellow. More days pass and asters bloom. The purples of the asters and the yellows of the goldenrod vibrate against one another, making the fields look as if they are in motion even on still days.

For some reason I had the telephone company put in a red phone. I think of it as a hot-line phone, the kind that sits on a desk in a radio station's newsroom, or in a president's boudoir beside his bed. In the past I've always had black phones that quickly became invisible in their surroundings, camouflaged by familiarity. A red phone is different. My peripheral vision keeps insisting on picking it up no matter where I'm standing in the kitchen, whether I'm searching for mayonnaise in the fridge or squatting to watch a cake rising in the oven through the window in its door. I keep expecting to actually *see* it ring, to see it do a little dance, a jig, while it jangles, as phones do in cartoons. I know this is just a trick of my mind, but that is no help to me.

What I really don't want is to appear pushy. Men, I've found, don't go for pushy women. But it's hard waiting and I find I can't concentrate properly on my work. It's like when you're watching a pot of water with an egg in it that you intend to soft-boil, waiting for the tiny bubbles to get big enough so you can start timing it, so it will come out absolutely perfect, the only way you like it, and while you're waiting you can't do anything else. The phone waiting is just like that, only worse.

I take the phone off the hook when I go to town to shop so I won't miss his call. I cruise the highway slowly, hoping to see something on the shoulder that I can bring to him. One day my hopes are raised for a moment only to be dashed the next when the dark object I'm approaching turns out not to be the body of—oh, it would have been sweet—a turkey vulture, but only the shredded remains of a transport truck tire. Hell, I would have settled for a grackle, or even a red-winged blackbird. For a measly starling I would have danced a fandango down the centre-line.

When I'm good and unhappy, what I think is a miracle happens. Don't laugh. I'm sitting in the living room staring out into the fields, watching the sun set, thinking, Yeah, yeah, yeah, yet another stunningly beautiful sunset, how boring, because I'm alone and beauty is nothing if you have no one to share it with, when this football comes out of nowhere, out of the pink instead of out of the blue because that's the colour of the sky. I see it as a brown blur heading straight at the window. It happens too fast for me to get out of the way, but my hands have a mind of their own and manage to reflex themselves over my eyes.

It sounds like an explosion when the window implodes. Sharp shards of glass embed themselves into the backs of my hands, making them tingle as if they're going to sleep, nipping at them with tiny pointed beaks. Cool dusk air fills the room.

When I take my hands away from my eyes I see that it's not a football lying on the carpet at my feet, but a pheasant, a resplendent male, brilliant red flesh around his eyes, his iridescent head green as chromed moss. Dead as a doornail. I feel an instant sorrow for him, then elation.

"Oh, thank you god," I say aloud—I, a non-believer, a solid atheist, except at small moments like these when I am strangely and strongly devout.

I am, in my imagination, already standing at his door, knocking, proffering this, my gift to him. I see his scar shift shape with his smile.

In real life my hands are under the bird. Its weight is less than I would have imagined, its feathers softer. My heart is pounding out a rejoicing hosanna when one of the bird's eyes opens. Naturally, my first thought is that the corpse has been suddenly possessed by a demon, a mean-spirited demon out to spoil my happiness. This impression passes quickly as I watch the eye roll backward, then forward, then around, until finally the pupil finds equilibrium in the centre. The eye stares up at me, the exact same jewel I've seen in my taxidermist's special eye case, except that this one has that added, inimitable glint of life.

I'm contemplating wringing the bird's neck when it suddenly wrestles itself free from my hands, wings thrashing. Loose feathers flutter out from it as it takes loud flight, hurls itself into the wall beside the broken window, falls to the carpet, is up again and out of the window and my life before I have a chance to get to my feet.

There is nothing for me to do but sit there on the carpet and pick the slivers of glass from my hands. It feels as though I'm plucking feathers, one by one, from two oddly shaped birds.

You'd think I'd give up. Especially after I see him with someone else. And it's not even in the local greasy spoon, where it could just be that they're platonic friends sharing a cup of coffee. It's in the IGA and they're shopping for groceries together. I stay a safe distance away from them while they're in the produce section discussing the merits of a particular green pepper—at least, that's what I imagine they're doing. The way they're handling the pepper also looks somewhat sensual to me, which makes me angry.

She is wearing pink. Everything she has on is pink. Pink is a colour I have never included in my wardrobe. It suddenly occurs to me that I have made a major life mistake. Can you believe it? Sometimes the human mind is a thing of wonder.

I skirt through pickles and relishes and mustards in a fury, the wheels of my cart rattling loudly on the terrazzo floor. I forget the butter I really need. I throw two bags of miniature marshmallows into the cart. Marshmallows! It's while I'm standing indignantly in the 8 Items or Less line that he taps me on the shoulder, a tap that cuts through my body to the very centre of my being, as a laser might, or Cupid's arrow.

"Haven't seen you lately," he says. There she is, standing behind him, smiling as if she is a nice person.

"No," I say, "I've been rather busy." *Rather?* I must be out of my mind to use a word like that.

"Drop by sometime," he says, smiling, warm. "I'm doing a pheasant." And he winks at me. "Sally here found it. Sally...," he says, "this is Rachel." One of those over-the-shoulder introductions. "She's just down the road from you. I'm surprised you two haven't bumped into each other before."

"It was lying dead in my vegetable garden," Sally pipes up. "In the carrots."

"That's nice," I say, trying to smile, but my mouth feels all crooked, my upper lip sticking to one of my front teeth.

"Weird though," he says. "Had to pick bits of broken glass out of its feathers...but what did I tell you about getting the eyes first, eh?"

Good Christ. It's not just the mind that's a thing of wonder, sometimes it's the world.

26

In the car I embrace the steering wheel, rest my head on my arms, and count the number of vehicles in the parking lot that have men sitting in the driver's seat waiting for their wives to finish shopping. I try explaining to myself that I shouldn't be too upset about the Pink Woman finding *my* pheasant, the pheasant *I* was going to give him. I mean, if you think about it, it was really *his* pheasant. He was the one who bought the eyes. She didn't steal it from me.

But my rational mind is connected to my emotions at best only tenuously. So I find myself driving down the highway, then up the highway. In desperation I follow the wonky curves of the lake roads, criss-cross the countryside on the concessions. I go up hills, I swoop down into valleys. I'm looking for something to hit. It's my only chance now.

A deer would be good. He'd like a nice, big deer. Or something exotic and uncommon, like a lynx. I've never even seen a lynx, not even in a zoo, but by god, if I see one now I will run it down, slow down enough to give it just the gentlest kiss of the bumper, so that while it arcs up and away from the car its neck will snap and it will land dead, but unmarked, in the gravel. I am absolutely convinced that I can do this. I who, for moral reasons, haven't touched meat, haven't eaten even a nibble of bacon, my favourite food, in six years.

I'm on the Twin Lakes road when my chance comes. The grasses sprouting from the edge of the shoulder are yellow and dry and at one point I see movement where they join the ground, something small and brown. It darts into the open.

Who do I think I'm kidding? I have no real choice. I brake. I brake to a full stop.

It's a moment before I understand what kind of creature it is that's scurrying across the road. It's a weasel, I know that— rusty brown above, white below, tiny short legs—but it's as if I'm seeing double: there are too many tails, too many heads. Six legs? I'm sure there are six legs running in synchronized step, two tails held aloft, and two heads, definitely, one looking right, the other left. No trick of the eye, or the mind.

Without question it's a Siamese twin weasel that disappears into the grasses on the other side of the road. The kind of thing a taxidermist would kill for. And I have spared it.

I cruise back out onto the highway and head north. The sun is setting, gilding the hay stubble in the fields. I don't want to watch the road; looking at the road is making me nervous, it's making me feel as if the very act of watching it will force something to run into my path that I will be unable to avoid. It feels safer to stare at the car's shadow racing alongside me. The sun is so low that its yellow rays are cutting right under the belly of the car, delineating even the wheels. The car's shadow speeds by big and fast on the hedges, then *zing*, it's suddenly a tiny little thing floating along way out there in the fields. Close up, then far away, then close up.

Watching it, being part of it, makes me feel as if I'm floating, as if the tires of the car aren't even touching the asphalt, as if I'm in the middle of an out-of-body experience that both the car and I are sharing.

I start singing, for no good reason at all, and then I start waving at our shadow, the car's and mine, just to make movement inside its movement, to make it look as if it's not the shadow of something inanimate, to prove that I'm there and here at the same time. It suddenly seems awfully funny and I start to laugh, then I'm laughing and waving with both hands at once, the shadow so close and clear at times that I can count my fingers, all ten of them.

Goldfish

I found myself on the couch downstairs in the living room, shivering stark naked. The light was on. The green numbers on the VCR said 4:52. A towel was on the floor. For a soothing moment, like the first waking memory of a really weird dream, it all seemed perfectly normal.

I was cold. Beside the couch where I lay curled up in goosebumps, the filter in the fish tank hummed loud as a refrigerator. Air bubbles burst on the surface of the water, I could hear them, even through the chattering of my teeth. I reached out and grabbed the towel, draped it around myself. It was old, coarse-textured, and not very warming.

I should be in bed, I thought, in bed, in bed, but I just lay there shivering. It occurred to me that I ought to be questioning what I was doing naked in the living room in the middle of the night, but it seemed too challenging a problem to tackle. I glanced at the fish tank instead. Sputnik was a large goldfish and I should have been able to see him instantly. I pulled myself closer. *Blub-lub*, the water plants swayed around the bubbles. There was no other sign of life in the tank, there was no fish.

Alertness entered my body like a drug I hadn't planned on taking. I must have sleepwalked. Maybe I ate my fish in my sleep, let him slither down my dreaming throat. Was that a flutter of fins I felt in my stomach? Or fear?

I peered over the arm of the couch. There he was, lying on the carpet, unmoving, opalescent orange on early-morning blue shag.

I want you to know that I'd had that fish for more than two and a half years.

Once a year, in May, the Portuguese church around the corner is transformed for its spring festival. Christmas-light crosses and flowers illuminate its façade, hundreds of winking lights trace up and down its spire. The surrounding streets are garnished with decorated poles joined one to the next by strings of coloured flags and streamers riffled by the breeze. A flowered gazebo, where bands can play even in the rain, is erected on the south lawn of the church, and on the remaining grounds a variety of tableaux are arranged. One of these tableaux consists of a man, a plough, and a shoddy replica of an ox. The man is a mannequin dressed in ill-fitting clothes. He is missing several fingers. The wounds do not heal from one year to the next; rather they get worse, like leprosy.

Behind the church, the tarmac of the school is turned into a fairground faster than seems possible. Friday afternoon the trucks roll in, gears grind, backup beeps beep, tents unfold, and by dinnertime rides are already swinging squealing kids within inches of the windows they stare out of in boredom the rest of the year. Glistening wieners turn on stainless-steel rollers, stray candy floss sticks to the soles of shoes or becomes matted in hair, and carnival hucksters, the usual motley assortment of toothless youths with drug-glazed eyes, loudly offer wonky-weighted darts to passersby—hit a red star in the middle enough times and you too could win a mirror screen-printed with the logo of a popular American brand of beer.

In the centre of all this action is the goldfish game. On a low, square platform, small-mouthed, spherical glass bowls are neatly arranged in concentric circles. Each bowl is filled with coloured water, and swimming or floating in each is a single tiny goldfish. For a buck, a woman who has a skin condition that allows only one side of her face to tan gives you seven ping-pong balls. Toss one in a bowl, win a goldfish.

Frank and I decided that it was imperative that we save at least one of the fish. It took eight dollars' worth of ping-pong balls, but we finally bounced one into a bowl of fuchsia-coloured water.

When the woman with the two-tone face handed us the bowl we'd won, we questioned her about the occupant's health. She told us that she had a huge tank in her trailer, filled with hundreds of fish. She bought them from a supplier for a penny apiece. At this price, the supplier guaranteed that the fish were free of disease.

"We treats them good," the woman said. "Normal water, like, in the big tank." She pointed at the display bowls. "Not to say that colour there is bad for 'em. It's just like what they uses on birthday cakes."

Apparently she was right. Not only did Sputnik survive, he thrived. Four inches long by now, he lay stiff and sticky in my hand. His long, elegant tail was encased in a sheath of cat hairs. He must have thrashed for a long time, flopping about on the blue shag rug.

Although I was sure there were little X's in his eyes, I decided to try artificial respiration anyway. I rushed him to the kitchen sink and turned on the tap to a gentle trickle and let the water run over his gills. The cat hairs slid off and disappeared down the drain.

Sputnik had not been the most entertaining living companion I had ever had, but I had grown fond of him.

"Breathe," I whispered. "Breathe, goddammit." But nothing happened. His eyes remained static.

For fifteen minutes I urged him to breathe. His orange scales were so desperately beautiful that I refused to give up on him. But it was late at night and I was weary. I had sleep-walked for the first time in my life and my feet were freezing. The tiles of the floor were so cold they could have been cemented onto a block of ice.

To keep myself awake, I began planning Sputnik's burial. I would put him in a zip-lock bag in the freezer and when spring came, when the soil was workable again and there were tulips and narcissi to decorate his grave, I would thaw him and bury him in the back garden. Maybe on Festival Weekend.

That would be fitting. I was nearing tears. The cat sidled into the kitchen and rubbed her warm fur around my legs.

For a brief instant I believed I saw one of Sputnik's gills flutter, but decided upon reflection that it was a simple hallucination. I stared at my fingers. They had turned into albino prunes. I thought I saw Sputnik's gill flutter again. It seemed quite impossible, but I was sure it did. And then the gill quite plainly flipped open, quivered, then closed again.

My heartbeat quickened. After several more minutes, Sputnik was breathing steadily, even when I held him an inch beyond the flow of the tap. I felt like a medic or a fireman returning to someone the gift of life. It was a grand feeling. Sputnik flopped briefly in my hand. I filled a mixing bowl with bottled water and placed him in it. He lay on his side floating on the surface, laboriously moving his gills, but he was alive.

With morning came a vague memory of tragedy. I had dreamt Sputnik had jumped from his tank and onto the living-room floor. This I found to be true when I saw him swimming in slow circles in the mixing bowl in the kitchen. He was not quite right, still a little off keel, but much better than dead.

But I had also dreamt that Frank was seeing someone else. Behind my back, the swine. I accused him of this. I told him my dream.

"You're mad at me because of a dream?" he asked, incredulous. "A dream! For god's sake," he said, "you've gone loopy on me." He stirred his coffee with a spoon. Frank never stirs his coffee. Frank drinks his coffee black, taking neither cream nor sugar, so why was he stirring his coffee with a spoon?

"Good thing for Sputnik you walked in your sleep last night," he said. "Guess you're psychic or something, eh?" He put the spoon down.

I tried hard not to be, but I couldn't help being affected by the dream. I still felt as if I had been betrayed, especially since I kept getting flashes of Frank's face pressed against some strange woman's. At odd moments I would even smell her perfume. But after a few days the realness of it passed, as the memories of dreams always pass, into that gauzy place dream-memories are held, until I could only remember the memory of the dream and not the dream itself.

The annual spring festival came and went. Sputnik recuperated completely and continued to grow. He leapt out of the water often. After his near-death escapade, we put a piece of screening over the top of the tank so he couldn't escape. I watched him sometimes leap high enough out of the water that his dorsal fin, even his slippery back, bumped against the wire mesh. Water splashed against the wall and made blisters in the wallpaper.

It happened so frequently that I began to wonder if Sputnik was trying to commit suicide each time he thrust himself out of the water and into the air. Had it been a conscious effort to end his life the night I found him on the carpet? Or simply a cry for help? Had I been wrong to meddle? Even if he was only a fish? I became racked with guilt over these questions and finally convinced myself that Sputnik was a terribly unhappy fish.

"Let's take him to the fishpond in Allan Gardens," I suggested one Saturday morning. Frank was groggy. He'd come home late the night before, had had extra work to do.

"It'll be an expedition, an adventure," I said, to rustle up some enthusiasm.

"Okay," he said, "in a little while." Frank seemed drained to me, sapped of energy, not quite his normal self, but a couple of coffees perked him up.

I love the way the humidity hits you when you walk into the palm-tree house, and the alien pollens and smells. I was carrying Sputnik in a plastic bag filled with water from his tank.

"It's okay," I said with forced conviction. "You're going to love it here. Honest."

The goldfish pond is in the camellia and English ivy house. The air there is as humid as in the palm-tree house, but cooler. Water drips onto moss-covered rocks. At the far end is the pond, small, but a charming place for a goldfish to retire. There's a Leda and the Swan statue presiding over the pond. Leda holds a ewer that spills a steady stream of water into the pool. The swan's neck is bent, his beak partially open, frozen forever in such a way that it looks as if he wants to drink from the trickle, or to snap at it if it gets out of line. That day, the spilling water reminded me of when I ran the tap water over Sputnik's gills and brought him back to life. I was suddenly confused. Was I doing the right thing? Or was this another mistake?

"Frank?" I said. "Could you do it?"

He took the plastic bag from me. Sputnik thrashed for a moment, then settled down. Frank squatted beside the pool.

"Okay, sport," he said. "This is it."

My throat and stomach suddenly constricted with a feeling of dread, of impending doom, as if the physical nature of the universe were about to be irreparably altered and I alone would be responsible.

Carp mouths sucked at the surface of the water. Frank untwisted the twist-tie. The water began to spill out, but Sputnik swam against the flow, obviously not sure that he wanted to follow it out of the bag. And then out he slid. With a wet plop, he slipped from one world into another, like Alice stepping through the looking-glass. For a moment he seemed disoriented, hung still just below the surface, but then he rallied and darted under an overhanging ledge.

Frank put his arm around my shoulder and squeezed.

"Well," he said. "Are you okay?"

I was impressed by the soothing tone of his voice, the sensitivity it implied. Maybe he really was the man I'd have a family with.

"Let's wait a minute," I said. I wanted to see Sputnik swimming free before we left. We stayed ten minutes or so. Nothing happened. Sputnik didn't come out of hiding, the world didn't end. We made it as far as the palm-tree house before I burst into tears.

That summer, whenever we rode past Allan Gardens on our bikes, I would always honk my horn. I'd ask Frank to ring his bell. Maybe Sputnik would hear, maybe not. Frank thought this was completely insane, but he indulged me. I visited Sputnik, sometimes alone, sometimes with Frank. Frank, I think, was more fond of our fish than he cared to let on—you know how men are.

It was not hard to recognize our goldfish. He was the one who was completely orange except for a dime-size white spot centred in the middle of his back. Sometimes, when the light hit him just right, the spot even looked silver. Also, his tail was more extravagant than any of the others.

I would bring him dried ground shrimp treats. For some strange reason, the manufacturer of these things even shaped them like shrimps. They floated on the surface of the pool, flesh-coloured commas, and drew a crowd of sucking and nibbling mouths.

Frank told me that I had walked in my sleep again. He heard noises downstairs in the middle of the night. At first he thought it was an intruder, then he realized I was not in bed beside him. He found me in the kitchen, running water over my cupped hand. He said that at first he thought I looked like Lady Macbeth. He was a little spooked until he heard what I was saying.

"Breathe, goddammit, breathe," I repeated over and over again.

Frank steered me back up to bed without waking me. I have no memory of this at all.

That dream I had foreshadowed the truth. Frank was seeing someone else. Too many late nights, too many wrong numbers hanging up on me, too many days he was cheerful as a lark, flushed with that look newly pregnant women get, or people who have fallen newly in love. Also, Frank was nicer to me than usual, more tolerant of my quirks, my foibles. This clinched my suspicions. I'd read Ann Landers. I knew the signs. Sorrow and a heavy emptiness in my stomach were my constant companions.

The house became smaller and smaller when Frank was not there; I used to think it was a big house. I took to sitting in restaurants and cafés writing cheerful letters to friends, hoping they would somehow sense the unhappiness I was unable to put into words. I rode my bike around the city, aimlessly, hoping the exercise would help release from my body the toxins caused by negative emotions. I swam through the traffic.

I saw Frank with the other woman. I didn't know who the hell she was, I had never seen her before, but Frank had brought her to see Sputnik. I could not believe this audacity, this duplicity, this betrayal. Him bringing her to see our fish was a violation of all kinds of things, as bad, maybe, as inviting her to use my toothbrush, or climbing into bed with me while still redolent of her smell. This finally brought anger to me.

Seething with rage, I spied on the two of them through the camellias. My heart was pounding so furiously that my temples and the sides of my neck were pummelled by my own blood. The rush of a non-existent waterfall filled my ears. I watched Frank put his arm around this woman, watched his hand squeeze her shoulder, as they gazed down into the pool. I knew they were looking at Sputnik through a reflection of themselves.

I snuck away before they saw me, backtracked through the palm house, past the banana trees, all the way to the cactus house, where the dry, hot air let me breathe more normally again. Maybe I was sleepwalking and this was just a dream. I ignored the sign that said Do Not Touch and reached down to a long-spined cactus, jabbed my palm hard into its needle-sharp points. This action didn't wake me; it drew a drop of blood from my lifeline, it loosed the tears from my eyes, but it didn't wake me.

I knew what I had to do, but I could hardly unlock my bike because the steady flow of tears was screwing up my sight. It was probably the tears too that made me blithely ride into an opening car door on my way home. My bike stopped quite suddenly but inertia insisted that I continue, now in flight. I sailed up and over the door, completely weightless, so slowly that I saw everything, so slowly that I had time to make rhythmic but futile gropings in the air before I returned to the ground.

I landed on my back on the pavement, the wind knocked neatly out of me. A streetcar rumbled by, very loudly, jostling the pavement like a mild earthquake. It was a long time before I could draw in a breath. A man was looking down at me, his lips moving, but all I could hear was a deep resonant ringing in my ears.

When I had recovered, I mounted my bike again and continued home. I picked up Sputnik's old scoop net and a plastic bag, then pedalled back to Allan Gardens.

Frank and the woman were gone. Sputnik was swimming slow circles in the middle of the fishpond. I filled the plastic bag with water and then, with surprisingly little trouble, scooped up Sputnik with the net and wrangled him into the bag.

The pebbles on the beach down by the waterworks are multi-coloured. The wet ones, lacquered by waves at the water's edge, are so beautiful they could be polished pieces of amber or amethyst or bloodstone. I have always loved that beach. Frank and I used to go for walks there and have picnics perched on sun-bleached driftwood. I used to imagine that we would bring our kids there and search with them for trilobites and gold.

The plastic bag Sputnik was in was opaque so I couldn't see him, could only feel the sloppy weight of the water. I had no idea if this was the right thing to do, but it felt right. Even if he only lived the summer, it would still be an adventure for him. After all, he was a carp, a survivor. I took off my shoes and socks and waded a couple of feet into the lake, carrying Sputnik in the bag.

When I released him, he didn't dash off immediately. He stayed instead in one position, confused perhaps by the alien movement of the water, the thrust towards the beach of the waves above, the swing of the undercurrent in the opposite direction. His fins fluttered, his flamboyant tail waved. Tentatively he swam forward a few inches, and then a few inches more. Do goldfish feel fear? I wondered. Was Sputnik as afraid as I was? And then he was gone.

Insects whispered above my head. Lake Ontario licked its shore. I sat on the dry pebble beach for a long time, until imprints of the stones were left on my thighs, even through my jeans. I lay back and stared up at the clouds sweeping slowly east, waiting expectantly for one of them to split apart, waiting for a big net to appear, to scoop me up and transport me to some other place, a place where I would be free of this anger, this throbbing sorrow, this pain. I stared at the clouds until it was me who was moving and not them, until I was floating in the opposite direction, effortlessly swimming against the rotation of the earth.

Pinned

It was stinking out the day Martha met Bobby's Uncle Roy and fake uncle, Ron, both she and Lydia agreed. They'd spent the worst of it, the midday hours, surrounded by the smell of Tide and Bounce in the dank cool of Lydia's parents' basement, working on perfecting their pool game. Lydia, living with the table, was still Martha's superior, particularly on long corner shots that she banged straight in, but Martha was picking up the nuances of the game fast and seemed to have a natural proclivity for those tight-angled side pocket shots. Lydia, who had been playing going on two whole years, had been getting more and more annoyed watching Martha tap the chalked tip of her cue so lightly onto the cue ball for those hard-to-get shots that Lydia felt like egging the damn thing on so it would at least touch whichever ball she'd called on it to hit, just so's she wouldn't scratch, because scratching was a drag. But then, more often than not it would make contact, sending that second ball rolling along so slowly Lydia would have plenty of time to see that it was right on the money before it sliced neatly into the side pocket with what must have been, for Martha, a gratifyingly sweet *plump*. And, dammit, Martha'd only played maybe a total of eight times. So Lydia, feigning boredom, had called an end to it by suggesting they cruise over to the quarry for a swim.

"Okay," said Martha. "Let's."

It was going on four, sun still high, not even an insinuation of a breeze. They were both wearing their bathing suits under oversized T-shirts, their legs bare almost to their bums. It had not rained recently but the township grader had done all the concession lines anyway, so as the girls walked they skidded occasionally on loose gravel and dust puffed up around their feet. By the time they came up to the Paynes' first open field past their maple bush, both girls' ankles were socked in beige powder. Roy's truck, an older model baby blue Dodge, was parked in the field facing the road, its box stacked high with the first hay, as was a flatbed trailer hitched behind it. Square bales. Roy and Ron were probably the only farmers within a fifty-mile radius who hadn't yet switched over to round. Two people were leaning against the front of the truck, a third was perched between them on the hood. A pop can being raised to a mouth flashed in the sun.

"It looks like both of them," Lydia whispered although they were nowhere near close enough yet for anybody to hear. "That's weird."

Everyone—including Martha and Lydia, who at fourteen believed themselves worldly—knew that although the two Payne brothers lived in the same house, they did not share the house. They each had separate apartments, Roy the downstairs, Ron the upstairs. Ron had welded the crude fire-escape steps that led to the upper west window himself. He had never bothered to convert that window into a real door, only used it as one. It was an old sash window, as all the windows in the house were. He just slid it up and slithered in or out, always feet first.

Not only did the brothers not share living quarters, it was rumoured that they never spoke to one another, not a single word for the past eight years. No one had any real idea what had precipitated this state of affairs but there was plenty of conjecture. Some people hypothesized that since both Paynes had had a thing for Eileen when they were boys—that was no secret—it had to have something to do with her, but someone else would always point out that that just wouldn't wash, the three of them had lived perfectly happily together in that very same house, actually sharing it, for what? It had to be ten years after Roy and Eileen got married. Obviously then, someone else would interject, it had something to do with money, not a far stretch when the interjector knew that in his own life money was always at the heart of unmendable family rifts. Or maybe, just maybe, another theory went, it was Ron getting worse, you know, after his accident, like maybe the brain damage was spreading. Something like that could happen, couldn't it?

Martha knew Roy by sight, but Ron only by legend. Ron never came into town. Maybe he had before he'd hurt his head, but that was before Martha could remember.

"Have you ever met him? Ron?" Martha asked, thinking that, them being half-mile-apart neighbours, it was a possibility.

"Nope. Just seen him."

"I've never even seen him," said Martha.

"Well, it's both of them, all right," said Lydia as they got closer. "Them and"—she was squinting, trying to make out the third—"ooh, it's Bobby."

Bobby was the one with the pop can. It was Pepsi.

"Yo," he said, raising the can a couple of inches in greeting when the girls had come up even with them.

Both Roy and Ron, leaning against the headlights on either side of Bobby, nodded once in acknowledgement of the girls' presence. Ron's eyes narrowed in shamelessly on their bare legs. Martha felt self-conscious about her lack of tan more than anything.

"Getting in the hay, eh?" said Lydia.

Ron, not taking his eyes off the lower regions of the girls, rubbed his chin on his shoulder, the kind of movement a cow might make. His face, like those of the other two, was masked in particles of hay, splinters, and dust plastered on with sweat.

"Going to the quarry?" said Bobby.

"Yeah." It was Lydia who answered although the question had been aimed at Martha. Bobby had never spoken to Martha before and his speaking now had made her suddenly too shy to respond. Bobby was sixteen.

Martha looked down and bothered a bird's-foot trefoil

with the toe of her sneaker. A bumblebee flew off. The yellow flowers continued to joggle for several moments after she took her foot away. She looked up again, caught Bobby staring at her.

"Maybe I'll meet you there," he said. "We'll be done after we unload. Right, Uncle Roy?"

"Yup. You can tell your Uncle Ron I said so."

Slyly smiling beyond the peripheral vision of either of the older men, Bobby shimmied his eyebrows for the girls.

With Herculean effort Martha and Lydia controlled themselves until they'd almost reached the Paynes' drive, where, clutching one another's arms to keep from falling in the gravel, they bust loose into laughter.

"Bizarre or what?" said Lydia when she felt capable of speech again.

"They really don't talk to each other!" said Martha. "Can you believe it?"

"I don't know how Bobby can stand it when he's here."

"Guess he's used to it, I guess."

Coming up even with the drive, they both pointed at the mailboxes at the same time. There were two. One said Roy Payne, the other Ronald. Roy's was a regular older hardware-store model on a cedar post, Ron's a rusted metal box fixed to a welded snake of thick, equally rusted chain. The girls lost it again.

"Guess they gotta each have their own IGA flyer every week," sputtered Lydia.

"And Home Hardware," said Martha, barely able to get the words out.

"And Zellers!" Lydia couldn't stand it.

When she was composed enough, she wiped her eyes with the towel she'd been carrying slung around her neck. "There's supposed to be another one, too," she said. "Up by the house. They leave notes for each other. Put the flag up so they know."

"Get out. I never heard that before."

Martha stared towards the house, looking for it. Bobby's Chev was there in the drive, parked in the shade of one of the Manitoba maples. Two separate clumps of peonies on the front lawn had been freshly mowed around. In the fallow field beside the drive, an automotive and agricultural history of the farm poked up through the tall grasses and weeds: the rounded lines of a red International; rusted farm machinery; the roof of a sixties boat of a car; a Leaning Tower of Pisa outhouse; asparagus fronds; a single rhubarb plume; an ancient contorted apple tree. An orange and white cat lolled in one of the tree's crooked elbows. Beyond were the barns. But Martha saw no mailbox.

"Where?" she said.

"I don't know, but it's true. They're wacko. Especially Ron. Did you see his eyes?"

"Yeah. No kidding," said Martha.

They passed two more fields before they hit the cedar swamp. It was so dense and dark in there that they could feel cooler air seeping out from between the straight, hairy trunks of the cedars and onto the road. It smelled different, too. Keenly resinous compared to the sweet, soft mustiness of the dried hay.

"Spooky," said Martha.

Which reminded Lydia: "Have you finished *Communion* yet?"

Communion was the Witley Strieber book that was being passed around. Everybody had already seen the video, but the book, they all agreed, was more powerful, mostly because it was easier to empathize with the guy in the book than with that creepy Christopher Walken guy.

"Yeah, a couple of days ago," said Martha. "It was great. That being paralysed and not being able to move but knowing those little alien guys are doing all that stuff to you, that's so cool."

"Cool but scary."

"Yeah, scary, but *way* cool. So have you looked for scars on you? You know, the little scars they leave on your neck or back?"

"No," Lydia sneered, twisting her face as she twisted the word, an appropriate response to what she considered an accusation of deviant behaviour she wished she'd thought of first.

"I did," said Martha, boasting. "I used a mirror to look all over me."

"And, well?"

"Well nothing. Too bad, eh?"

They walked on in silence, Lydia thinking only briefly about alien abductions before returning to where she'd been a few minutes before, imagining herself with Bobby in the barn, surrounded by the smell of tack and horses and saddle soap. Martha was elsewhere, staring with unfocused eyes into the brush beyond the turn ahead, thinking about being paralysed and having things done to her. Aliens doing those things was only a small twist on a theme she had, despite her youth, spent time with already.

A year before, she and a bunch of other kids had been playing a kind of hide-and-go-seek game in a cornfield on the edge of town. It must have been fall because the cornstalks were dry and rattled whenever they were bumped into. Night had fallen while they were out there, dusk anyway. One of the guys had caught Martha and thrown her down onto the dry, lumpy earth between rows. He lay on top of her, which she allowed because he was a boy she liked. She felt him weasel his hand up under her shirt, felt him grope at her breast through her bra. It was the first time she had ever let a boy do that so she lay very still. There was rustling in the cornstalks and another one of the boys came through.

"Hold her arms," said the first boy.

The phrase "No means no" came to Martha. "Hey," she said instead, simulating resistance as the second boy pinned her arms above her head.

The first boy was upright then, knees beside hers, but the bulk of his weight was on her shins. Martha couldn't move. The other boy roughly pulled up her T-shirt and started squeezing one of her breasts through her bra, fast, with fingers splayed, as if her breast was a pump and he was trying to inflate her.

"No, stop," she finally said when a third boy appeared, but because she was giggling she didn't really expect it to have any effect. She wasn't even convinced that she wanted it to; there was a frighteningly pleasurable buzzing between her legs. That was when she saw, between black-bearded ears of corn, her old best friend Natalie's startled face.

"But we *saw* you," Natalie had said a month later, when Martha had looked to her for comfort after finding some graffiti magic markered on the wall in one of the girls' cubicles, Martha's name and the word *slut* juxtaposed. She had already scratched it off with a penknife she carried in her bag, making a horrible nails-on-blackboard sound as the blade scraped the enamel paint down to the metal beneath. Band-Aid coloured paint that fell to the floor in fragile curls.

Martha was appalled, partly by Natalie's unconscionable lack of loyalty, but more by her naivety. Everyone knew a virgin slut was impossible; moreover, it was an oxymoron—she'd just learned what oxymorons were in Language Arts—so she'd done the only thing possible under the circumstances and dumped Natalie on the spot, and then, using lies about Natalie as gifts, courted Lydia and Angela as her new best friends. She'd had to do some regular scraping in the girls' washroom over the next couple of months, but the misused description of her, as far as she knew, had long since disappeared.

What hadn't disappeared, though, was the memory of being held down and the lusciously lubricating feelings that went with that memory. She invoked it regularly, usually at night in bed, her fingers slippery between her legs. From the beginning, she had cleverly erased the faces of the boys who had accompanied the original incident and substituted other faces in their place, Brad's for a while, then Leonardo's, and finally, since *Communion*, faces that had that classic, big-eyed alien look. She could just imagine their tiny, long-fingered hands touching her.

Another half-mile and they climbed over the fence where the biggest No Trespassing sign was wired on, a new one with a postscript painted by hand that said "Leave sign alone". Martha and Lydia knew that two similar signs were at the bottom of the quarry pond because they had seen them being thrown in the water.

On the trespassing side of the fence, cow vetch and yellow sweet clover crawled over the man-made ridge that had shielded the quarry from the road when it had been in operation. Martha and Lydia climbed over that hump before following a broad, flat limestone shelf towards the pit. Bonsai yellow hawkweed and viper's bugloss, wildflowers that had somehow found enough nourishment from a thin layer of gravel to bloom, brushed the road dust off the girls' ankles and calves as they walked. Heat radiated up from the pale, ash-grey limestone more intensely than from the road, so when they reached the huge chunks of fossil-encrusted rock that traced the top curve of the submerged ramp the trucks had at one time driven down, both girls wordlessly dropped their towels, stripped off their T-shirts, and dove off the opposite side into the cold turquoise water.

Although barely three hundred yards across at its widest, the pond was very deep, spring-fed, and most years never warmed up until mid-August, so when the girls resurfaced they screamed. A family of geese hugging the east wall turned their heads and peered towards the commotion. The goose and gander placed themselves between Martha and Lydia and their goslings, necks outstretched, daring them to come closer, relaxing only when they saw that the girls were not actually swimming towards them, but cutting a south-east diagonal through the water, heading for the cliff.

Bobby showed up about an hour later. They didn't hear his truck pulling into the gate, and he was barefoot, so his appearance from behind took both Martha and Lydia by surprise. They were on a limestone slab at the top of the cliff, Martha lying on her back with one arm draping her eyes, Lydia hunched beside her digging out running-shoe dirt from beneath her toenails with a tiny fossil clam.

It was the coolness of Bobby's shadow on her bare midriff that made Martha shift her arm up to her forehead, expecting to see a cloud. Bobby's head was haloed by the sun. She sat up—swanlike, she hoped.

"How long you been standing there?" she asked, squinting, still shielding her eyes from the sun.

"Wouldn't you like to know," he said.

Lydia, mortified, flicked her fossil pedicure tool out over the edge of the cliff. It was a moment before it hit the water, soundlessly leaving the same delicate rings on the surface as the toes of a dragonfly would. Lydia did not see that, though. She was staring at Bobby with doggy eyes.

He was wearing cutoffs now, must have changed out of his jeans at his uncles' place. Above the waist he was ghosted by hay dust. Shards and splinters were stuck all over his shirt and in his kinky hair, a single shred balanced on his eyelashes. Martha wanted to reach out and remove that one, but she didn't have the nerve. Bobby looked out over the water.

"Geese are still here," he said.

"Yeah," said Lydia. "The little guys are getting big. Are you going in?"

Martha was having trouble breathing with Bobby looming beside her. She could smell his sweat. For some strange reason, the smell didn't disgust her.

"Yeah. Are you?"

"Sure," said Lydia, "I'll go in again. You too, Martha?"

Martha didn't move, couldn't move. She was pinned by the smell of Bobby to the rock, pierced through the middle. She didn't move until the intimacy of him stripping his shirt off beside her embarrassed her over to the edge where Lydia was already waiting, posing, back slightly arched.

"On three?" said Lydia.

Martha nodded.

Bobby never simply jumped off the cliff, he did either back flips, front flips, or dives. He didn't have any particular finesse, but his nerve made up for his sloppy legs and splashy entries into the water. Whatever he did, it wowed the girls, although no matter where they were—treading water below, climbing up the natural stone steps of the cliff, or standing beside him waiting their turn at the top—they weren't about to let him know they were wowed. No way. Martha and Lydia were cool as cucumbers whenever Bobby grinned at them before he sucked in his breath and pounced fearlessly, like a puma, off the rock.

Lydia had just jumped and Martha, standing beside Bobby, was about to when she noticed his scar, a polished, hairless red arc that curved out from his armpit and over his breastbone. He caught her staring, compelling her to speak.

"What happened to you?" she asked. The instant the words had left her mouth, she realized she'd replaced them with her foot. It had been that awful car crash where Bobby's little sister had died. And Roy Payne's wife. Everybody knew Bobby didn't talk about it. Not ever. It was supposed to be an invisible scar.

"Oh, geez, I'm sorry," she said. What a first-class idiot she was. Below, Lydia was pulling herself out of the water.

Bobby ran his hand back through his hair, ponytailing it at the base of his skull and squeezing water from it. He had partially turned away from her so that, although she could no longer see the scar, she was able to watch the rivulet trace a path on either side of the sine wave of his vertebrae, pooling for a second on the waistband of his cutoffs before disappearing inside.

"I shouldn't have said anything," she said. She'd never felt so stupid. She wanted to touch him.

He looked at her. "Race you to the other side," he said.

Martha, knowing Bobby's dive would be deep, broke her own impact with her arms when she jumped so she would be the first to resurface, which gave her exactly what she expected, a head start and stinging armpits.

Although she was the better swimmer, Bobby was stronger and caught up quickly. Martha stepped up her pace, slowing only when she realized Bobby was matching her stroke for stroke, deliberately holding back so he was swimming even with her. When Martha flipped over on her back, where she leisurely fluttered her feet and hands, getting her wind back, Bobby broke out of his own crawl and fell into a slow, rhythmic breaststroke alongside her.

"You'd have beat me, anyway," Martha said. She could see Lydia up on the cliff, lying on her stomach on the tanning rock, ignoring them.

"Maybe," said Bobby.

"Definitely."

"There's the geese," said Bobby, gesturing ahead with his chin.

Martha rolled into a breaststroke to see. The family was following the contours of the far wall, edging away from the point the two of them were heading towards. They were both swimming in synch now, keeping their heads above the surface.

"I heard a goose at night once," said Bobby. "It was weird, because it was late. You don't usually hear them at night around here." He scooped up some water with his mouth, then fountained it out.

"That *is* weird," said Martha.

"I was lying in bed and I heard this honk. Then about five minutes later there was another honk. Maybe ten minutes later it happened again. Went on like that for about an hour. The thing just kept looping around, coming back over the house and honking. I figured it was lost."

Martha couldn't believe Bobby was telling her this. "That's sad," she said.

"Yeah, it was."

They were nearing the wall. The geese were long gone, were paddling and dabbling unconcerned over by the submerged ramp. Beside her, Bobby sucked in a breath and went down. Martha lost him for a moment in the reflection of the sun, but then she saw him again, swimming deep, kicking towards the wall. Watching his dark, sleek form shimmer away from her, Martha felt almost nauseated by what his very existence was doing to her.

Bobby gave them a ride back to Lydia's place. The girls sat on their towels so they wouldn't make the seat too wet. Lydia took the middle and prattled on so inanely for the five-minute ride that it seemed to Martha as if she were speaking in another language, a tongue Martha couldn't understand or, more precisely, didn't care to understand. Instead of listening, she stared at Bobby's hay-dusted jeans bunched on the floor at her feet, her thoughts swarming around his tragic story of the lost goose, approaching it from different angles, trying to find the meaning in both the story itself and the indisputable yet curious reality that he had actually told it to her. By the time they turned up Lydia's drive, Martha had convinced herself that the implications were profound.

The hanging branches of a weeping willow stroked the windshield just before they stopped. In the pasture, Lydia's horse, Babe, a chestnut gelding, lifted his head from grazing to watch. Two of the boarded horses, leaning against the miniature red barn, ignored them, tails swishing flies.

Martha leaned forward so she could see Bobby's face past Lydia's when she thanked him for the ride.

"No problem," he said. Nothing more.

Martha got out. She kicked some gravel at her feet, waiting for Lydia—wondering what Lydia was saying, alone with him in the cab, that she couldn't hear.

The girls watched the truck back out. They didn't wave as Bobby drove away; that would have been too corny. Only parents and little kids waved. When he was out of sight, Lydia grabbed Martha's arm, digging her fingernails into her biceps. "Guess what?" she said.

Martha was frightened by Lydia's radiance.

"He copped a feel," Lydia hissed, ecstatic.

A crushing weight seemed to be compressing Martha's lungs from above. "Where?" she asked. "When?"

"One of the times you were up at the top and me and Bobby were getting out. He grabbed my butt." Lydia whispered that last part forcefully, her neck aggressively outstretched, like one of the geese. "I knew he liked me. I *knew* it." Those words she barely said to Martha. She said them more like a prayer, a hallelujah. Martha felt like puking.

It wasn't until after they'd eaten a supper of frozen pizza pockets that Martha found the strength to ask Lydia if Bobby had said anything to her. They were in the basement playing pool again. Martha could hear Lydia's cat scratching the wall beside the litter box in the furnace room.

"No," said Lydia, miscalculating another bank shot. "He didn't have to." Her wayward striped ball, after missing the pocket, jostled Martha's four ball an inch out from the cushion, leaving it a forearm away from the side pocket. The cue ball finished a three-point bounce and settled into position near the four. A ridiculously tight shot. A shot only a fool would go for.

"Nothing?" said Martha, crouched over the table with her cue. No goose story? No nothing? She took aim, making sure. "He didn't say *anything* to you at all?"

"Uh-uh," said Lydia, reaching for the chalk.

Martha drew back her cue. She took a deep breath, then tapped the cue ball with such sudden confidence, such certitude, that she knew she didn't even have to look, that she could be anywhere with anybody, she could be pinned to a rock, she could be pinned to the sky and moon, and the four ball would still roll in.

Saint Francis and the Birds

I am not a religious woman. I suppose I have my parents to thank for that; they did not allow me to go to Sunday School as my best friend did. Instead, I was permitted to join the local Brownie troop, although I did not feel it was quite the same; the fairy mythology was not, to my eyes, the equal of the tales my friend brought home from church. She brought home, too, all manner of religious paraphernalia, the likes of which I had never seen before. I remember most clearly the cards she was given each week, small cards depicting saints in saintly pose, printed in rich colours, with scalloped edges and halos of gold.

One day, she showed me a Saint Francis of Assisi card. I had never heard of him, but coveted the picture because of the unusual addition of birds; I was fascinated, at the time, by birds. Not wanting to ask for it, in case she might refuse, I made a pretence later in the week to go into her room alone. I remember distinctly the way the card felt, sandwiched between my ankle and my sock, as I walked home that day, how the scalloped edges chafed my skin.

My parents were observant people and noticed my interest in birds. Telling me that birdwatching was a hobby, and that hobbies, like Brownies, were good for little girls, they bought me a pair of binoculars and the Peterson guide. So, early Sunday mornings, while my friend listened to Bible stories and coloured in pictures of Mary Magdalene, I would wander into the woods behind the pond. I would make myself perfectly still, binoculars poised at chin level, ready to focus on the slightest movement I saw in the branches above my head. I'd stalk birds for hours, noting their habits, ticking off warblers I'd never seen before in my guide, then memorizing their names. I would wear earth-tone clothes and move in three-inch increments, pretending I was a walking tree.

Years later, living in the city beside a park near Chinatown, I would watch nostalgically, alongside the pigeons and squirrels, old women doing their morning tai chi, moving as slowly and deliberately as I once had done when I was alone in the woods.

I am no longer a true birder—I do not go on seasonal counts and don't even know where my life list is—but I still notice, and even become excited, when a rarity to the city flies by. Just the other day, for example, as I was walking down the street, I saw a brown creeper scuttling like a crab up the trunk of a tree. I was on Queen Street and I was able to walk right up to within a yard of the bird, a forest bird. Streetcars rumbled by, and cars, and trucks. The creeper was not in the least concerned. I imagine it thought the flow of traffic was just some kind of river it had never seen before, and I'm sure it hadn't an inkling of what a human being was.

For ten minutes, I watched the bird eat white larvae. It pried them, quickly and precisely, out from under the bark, as if they were miniature noodles, using for chopsticks its curved needle beak.

I found the Saint Francis of Assisi door in the basement the day Ed and I moved in. It was a screen door, aluminum and cobwebby. In the middle of it, painted in enamel and raised in bas-relief, was a vulturous Saint Francis surrounded by birds, a sparrow feeding off his extended, open hand. I noticed that there was a living spider perched on the sparrow's head, like a crown.

I have seen many similar doors, but always decorated with more mundane imagery. Ducks, for instance, three ducks laid out in the same flight configuration as the plaster ones that used to hang, for sale, on hardware store walls.

I brushed the spider off the sparrow in Saint Francis of Assisi's hand and carried the door upstairs.

The house Ed and I had bought was a half-century old and half a mile from downtown. Attached to the north side, nailed onto the kitchen and back-room walls, was a crude pigeon coop. The coop had been built in such a way that it blocked the larger of the two kitchen windows—there was a small one in the back door—from the outside light. We would, I thought, standing in the kitchen with the Saint Francis door, be able to see into the coop when we ate.

Just then, Ed came into the kitchen. He looked at me and demanded to know what I thought I was doing with the door in my hands, saying there was a perfectly good one already out front. I was about to answer him when I was startled by something white fluttering in the coop. Ed saw it too. I leaned the door against the fridge and we both went outside.

One at a time, three pigeons flapped out of a hole in the door of the coop. They landed in a row on the red shingles of a neighbour's roof. They were pure white, all three of them. "Pigeons," Ed said. "We don't want pigeons." He opened the coop door, looked inside, then shut it again and closed the flap that was hinged to the entrance hole. He grunted, said it smelled like hell in there, and went back into the house.

I remembered half a jelly donut I hadn't finished eating during the move, and followed Ed in to get it. I came back out and threw some crumbs onto the lawn. It was late winter and there was still some snow in the backyard, half melted, made into crisp icing by the warming sun. Speckled city-black with grime, it was unpleasant and filthy, like old Styrofoam on a beach.

I watched the pigeons watching me, tilting their heads in interest from their perch on the neighbour's roof. I threw down more crumbs. First one pigeon and then the other two, barely moving their wings, wheeled down and landed in the sooty snow. I had never seen anything so white, white just this side of silver reflecting sun. I thought, How perfect: three white pigeons.

When the pigeons had finished eating and had flown away,

I brought the Saint Francis of Assisi door out into the yard and leaned it up against the back chain fence.

Later that same day, Ed pointed out what he called a rat hole under the kitchen sink. His facial muscles tensed and his jaw squared. I clenched my own teeth in sympathy and watched a vein in his temple throb.

We have a cat. His name is Phinny. He is a long-haired white cat, not deaf like most of his kind, perhaps because he has a black blaze on his chest. Phinny has an extra toe on each foot. This makes him look, I sometimes think, like a snowy owl when he pads around the tundra of our living-room carpet. We had him fixed when he was a child, which seems to have irreparably altered his personality. Most of the time, he has a dull, unfeline expression in his eyes. I often get the impression that he experiences no joy in life because of what we had done to him.

Ed brought Phinny into the kitchen and showed him the hole under the sink. In encouragement, he said, "Kill the rat, Phinny, kill the rat."

Gingerly, Phinny sniffed at the hole. He shook one over-sized paw and walked away.

Ed nailed the pigeons' entrance to the coop shut, but they came every morning anyway. I fed them. They were so pretty, so white.

A visiting friend told us that pigeons attract rats. Ed had not mentioned the hole under the sink. His face turned red. I saw the vein in his temple begin to throb again. The friend did not notice the change in Ed's expression and continued. The rats, he said, gnaw their way into pigeon coops and suck the eggs dry or eat the fledglings, chewing on their bones like barbarians. He laughed. I had a vision of the pigeons that had lived in the coop, panicking at the arrival of a rat. I could see them smashing against the windowpane, all feathers and wings, while the previous owners of the house sat eating at the table pushed up against the wall under the windowsill. I imagined the people as they continued to fork food into their mouths, ignoring the fracas, or perhaps watching it as if it were TV.

Ed borrowed a crowbar from the next-door neighbour and ripped down the coop. Multiple planks and rotting boards made up the floor, all sealed together with a mortar of pigeon droppings and feathers and the shells of broken eggs. Ed wore gloves and cursed loudly as he worked.

"There now," I said when he had done. We were both standing in the newly bright kitchen. "We won't have to worry about rats any more."

Ed just glowered at me and threw his work gloves into the garbage can. I tried to hug him, but he pushed me away. While he washed his hands, I stared out the back-door window at Saint Francis standing calmly at the end of the yard.

Feeding the pigeons in the mornings became, very quickly, part of my daily routine, like brushing my teeth and eating toast, before I went to work. I would go out into the yard and they would be waiting for me on the roof of the back room. They would slip down to the ground and I would feed them whatever stale bread or cake or even meatloaf we had on hand. The snow went away and for a short time they looked a little less perfect to me, less pure than before, pecking away at the soggy, yellow-brown lawn. But that feeling passed gradually, as the grass, day by day, became brighter green.

I remember, when I first moved to the city, I noticed the pigeons right away. They were uncommon where I came from. We had mourning doves instead. Every morning we would see them, and hear them cooing sadly on the telephone lines between the pines. It wasn't until I was thirteen that I found out what the word meant that I had thought was simply a misspelling of their name. By then I had lost a dog to a car and so could even make sense of it.

There is something virtuous and elegant, I think, about mourning doves, about all doves, something that pigeons lack. Doves, for instance, have such beautiful long and pointed tails, while pigeons' are blunt and squared. And of course it is pigeons, not doves, one sees along city sidewalks, with gnarled stumps at the ends of their pink ankles instead of feet. Sometimes, sitting in parks, I have seen the usual grey variety of pigeon close enough, and in the right light, to notice the colouring of their feathers, the iridescence, the play between purple and green on their necks. Those times, I have thought they were quite beautiful. But most of the time I cannot see that. I see them instead sitting in the middle of heavily trafficked streets, pecking at dirt and dried-up bubble gum, taking off at the last possible moment, making me think that I am to witness the death of a bird on my way home from work or going to the store. I look away.

My three white pigeons were not at all like those. They were too regal, too white. I preferred to call them doves. My three white, perfect doves, albeit with peculiarly stunted tails. I thought that, were he alive, Saint Francis at the end of the yard would agree.

Ed called Saint Francis of Assisi "Saint Frank". This might have offended me, were I a religious woman, but I am not.

Ed wanted to throw the door away. He called it an eyesore. I did not want to plead with him to let me keep it, so I suggested that the image of Saint Francis might act as a scarecrow, although I was sure he served more as an attractant than as a deterrent to the birds. In the end, Ed allowed me to keep him where he was.

By the end of March, my doves had become tame enough to eat from my hand. I never knew where they went for the rest of the day or where they roosted at night, but every morning they would drift down from the sky, like oversized flakes of snow. Ed said they were disgusting. He called them vermin and told me they had lice, but he could not convince me to give them up. He bought me a pair of gloves for my birthday, to wear while I fed them, but I used the gloves for gardening instead; I liked to feel the birds' scrawny feet on the bare palms of my hands, the delicate pecking of their beaks.

When they had gone for the day, other birds would come down to finish off their scraps. Starlings, for instance. Starlings are mimics. I have heard them repeat all manner of calls and songs other than their own coarse mutterings and squeaks. I think some of them must be immigrants from the north, from the woodlands and farms, where they may have come into contact with the birds whose songs they have stolen. Once, too, I heard a starling on a side street repeat over and over again, with great urgency, the clang of a street-car bell. Sometimes I have even thought I heard starlings speaking words, but I am probably mistaken about that.

Strange birds, birds not usually found in the city, began frequenting our backyard. One morning, before I was fully awake, I heard the song of a red-winged blackbird. It confused me, made me think I was fifteen again and late for school. When I realized where I was, I woke Ed and told him to listen to the song. "It's a red-winged blackbird," I said.

Ed was annoyed.

"It's spring," I tried again.

"No," he said, "it's six a.m."

Later, when a Baltimore oriole, bright orange and black, took a three-day rest in a neighbour's tree after its trip across the lake, I did not point it out to Ed—even when it landed on the top edge of the Saint Francis of Assisi door during dinner, in full view through the window of the back door.

It was Saint Francis, I knew, who, like a beatific magnet, attracted birds to my backyard.

In early April, mint began to grow around the base of the

Saint Francis door. It grew and grew. Mint is like a weed and will grow up through lawns and take over whole flower beds. There is nothing one can do about this because the plants have long, weaving, horizontal roots, roots that creep through the soil like worms. I do not like mint myself, but once in a while Ed would enjoy a few chopped leaves mixed with butter on his potatoes, so I let it grow.

Ed became convinced that we had rats in the house. He said he heard noises at night. He would take Phinny onto his lap after dinner and stroke him while whispering instructions in his ear. Phinny's ear would twitch as if a fly were wandering around inside, Ed would hold his lips so close. I did not think Phinny had it in him to confront a rat. I was sure he would run away, terrified. Ed, though, seemed to have faith, perhaps because the cat had once been the same sex as he. *I* did not believe we had rats.

I bought a bird feeder and hung it from a branch of a tree out back, so the birds that Saint Francis drew to the garden would have something to eat. In the month of April I saw an oven-bird, a brown thrasher, two evening grosbeaks (both male), another oriole, and a loud-mouthed, jeering blue jay, as well as the house sparrows and starlings that came every day in droves.

One morning, Ed read what I thought was a hysterical letter in the paper, suggesting that rats came into gardens late at night to eat the spilled seeds from bird feeders. Ed told me that that was it, the feeder would have to go. I ran into the backyard ahead of him and leaned against the trunk of the tree it was hanging from, my arms wrapped around it from behind, facing Ed. I felt like a Christian martyr even before he hit me. I am not a religious woman, but Saint Francis gave me strength. I watched Ed go back into the house. A sparrow landed on the ledge of the feeder still suspended above my head, knocking some seed to the ground.

Sometimes I would wear my dressing-gown in the back garden while I fed my doves. I would look to Saint Francis as if he were my reflection in a mirror, imitating his pose, hunched over with my open hand extended. Invariably, one of the doves would alight on my palm. One day I almost shaved the crown of my head, but I lost my nerve the moment I had the scissors in my hand. Ed had always admired my long hair, so I am sure not cutting it was the right decision to make.

It became warmer and we began leaving the front window open so that Phinny could go in and out as he pleased. One day, he brought in a rat. A young rat, a teenager I suppose. I was not home. Ed was. He told me afterwards, in a quiet fury, that the cat had come in with the rat in his mouth, its tail dragging on the carpet. Clumsily, stupidly, Phinny had let the rat escape. Ed finally trapped it in a corner. He said it jumped three feet straight up in the air, baring its teeth and squealing shrilly. Ed's upper lip contorted and I thought I saw it quiver before he continued. He told me that he finally trapped the rat by its tail with a shovel, then somehow managed to get an empty margarine container over it. He said it shrieked continuously until it had disappeared down the toilet which Ed had flushed just an instant before dropping it in.

Every now and then, for several weeks afterwards, I would find Phinny staring wistfully into the toilet bowl. I found this amusing. Ed did not.

One morning, not long after the incident with the rat, I was in the yard feeding my doves. One was on my shoulder, one was at my feet, and the third was pecking seeds from my hand. They rotated their positions in order, making me feel strangely as if I were juggling them, but in very slow motion. Ed came banging loudly out the back door and my doves flew away. I almost said something to him about frightening them, but the look on his face made me change my mind. He swore up into the sky, calling my doves "rats of the air". Then he stormed back into the house and slammed the door. I thought it best not to question this outburst and pretended it had not happened at all.

Later that same day, I looked out the back window and saw a ring-necked pheasant. It dashed under a car parked in the back lane.

Where I came from, there used to be hundreds of pheasants, vying with the rabbits to make the greatest number of footprints in the snow in our backyard. Their long tails would leave snake tracks behind them when they strutted at leisure, when the dogs were inside, but when they were in a hurry they bent forward, their tails in the air, like running lizards. In the fields I would sometimes come across them by accident in the high weeds, and five would fly up at once with a great racket of wings, so close that I could feel the change in the movement of the air, as if a fan had been turned on. But that morning it was a brown and orange cat that emerged from under the car, with not a white feather band around its neck, but a white plastic flea collar.

Ed tossed and turned in bed for several nights in a row. Finally, I asked him what was the matter. He raised himself up on one elbow and loured at me.

"I can still feel him," he said. "I can still feel him bumping against my hand through that goddamn margarine container." He spat the words down at me, as if I were somehow responsible for this memory of his. I lay very still and tried not to breathe while I waited for him to fall asleep.

When I was convinced there wouldn't be another frost, I began planting seedlings of annuals in the garden. I was happy to spend my free time out there with the birds, weeding and tending the lawn.

I did all the gardening. Ed would not come out into the backyard any more. I felt this was just his way of being tolerant of my quirks, of my feeding the birds. Occasionally, while

I was in the garden puttering around or standing with a dove in my hand, I would see him through the window in the back door, watching me. He never made any sign to show that he knew I saw him there. It felt odd at times, standing in the garden between my husband, staring at me from the kitchen, and Saint Francis, watching me protectively out of the corner of his eye.

One night in late May, as I lay unable to sleep in bed, I heard a sound in the walls, a gnawing sound, as if someone were eating a carrot made out of wood. I glanced at Ed lying silent beside me. I could see his open eyes reflecting a bathroom light from a neighbour's house.

"Squirrels," I whispered.

"Rats," he said.

I was awoken in the morning by the bang of the back door closing. Ed was not in bed beside me. I looked out the window, down onto the back-room roof and into the yard. It had rained. The greens of the immature leaves in the garden vibrated against the black, wet soil. Ed was standing in the middle of the lawn.

My three white doves were lined up on the roof of the back room, their backs to me. They were watching Ed. Ed held out his hand and opened it. I could see that he held something in his palm, seeds or beans. Saint Francis stood beyond him, against the fence, his hand extended in imitation of Ed's.

Ed clucked up towards my doves. They shuffled about on the shingles for a moment and then dropped off the edge of the roof, one by one. They fluttered down to him, briefly hovering above his head before landing in the wet grass at his feet.

I watched Ed feed my doves, my perfect doves.

By the time I got downstairs, Ed and the doves had gone. I found the box of rat poison in the back room. There were still some uneaten pellets on the lawn and I picked up as many as

I could find. I put them in the pocket of my dressing-gown.

I was about to go back inside when I heard the sound of wings above my head. I looked up just in time to see an osprey drop from a tree. It plunged, wings thrown back, down behind a garage into a neighbour's yard. There was a splashing sound and then I saw the bird rise again, toiling under the weight of a fish—a lake trout, I think it was. It kept losing altitude, then gaining it again, as the fish, not yet dead, struggled, drowning, in its claws. I watched the bird, with great flaps of its wings, disappear behind a house a few doors down.

I am not a religious woman but I know when to be grateful, so I glanced at Saint Francis to thank him for the osprey, although I knew there was nothing he could do about my doves. Looking more closely at him, I noticed that the rain had splashed some soil up onto him. I had to step in the circle of glossy green mint surrounding the door to get near enough to him with my sleeve. The smell of the crushed mint rose from my feet as I wiped the grime from his face and hands.

Waiting

Charlie and I went out parking the night his old man died, down where you could watch the slag being dumped. Everybody went there. It was as good a show as at the drive-in, only free.

You'd see it first, the molten rock flowing down the embankment a quarter-mile away, man-made lava pulsing orange in the twilight. I couldn't then think of anything more romantic.

The sound of its pouring always came a moment late, out of synch, like an echo of something you missed the first time around. But the best part, my favourite part, had always been the heat. It didn't hit sometimes until the first glowing trails had begun to fade to black, a sudden wall of hot air that seemed to have no attachment at all to where it was coming from. Sometimes the wall was broken into pieces by a cool evening breeze. When it was interfered with like that, it always made me think of swimming in a lake gone calm after a storm has passed, after the water's been churned by wind, the coldest parts from the deepest reaches, down where the lake trout hide, brought up top to mix with the sun-warmed parts. Swimming through first a patch of cold water, then a warm one, then a cold one again, like the lake's some crazy quilt of different temperatures.

Other times, the heat just came at you in one long, sexy wave. Those times it was like Charlie's breath, so hot against the cool skin of my neck, my throat, my arms, that I wanted it forever, I wanted him never to stop.

That night, like always, we stood in front of Charlie's truck while we waited for the first load to be dumped, me leaning back into him, resting my head on his breastbone. I could feel his breathing, could feel his heartbeat, his arms around me, his warm hands. We never talked while we were waiting, just stared up at the embankment trying not to blink too often, like when you're waiting for lightning during an electrical storm, or for shooting stars to fall. The sun had just slid down behind the smelter and the stacks were silhouetted black against the pinkness of the sky. I couldn't help but think how pretty a scene it was.

Charlie lit a smoke and we shared it, me still leaning into him, the ember glowing as orange as the slag was going to be every time I took a drag, as I stared beyond it towards the embankment. A bat dipped into sight. It swooped and swerved, tracing the same roller-coaster circuit over and over again while we waited.

I found a dead bat once at camp. It was the company camp. I was maybe ten.

It was free time before the breakfast gong and I was out back beyond the johns and generator looking for bear tracks in the sandpit, had been looking long enough that I was getting worried I might find some. I found the dead bat instead.

It was much smaller than I'd expected a bat to be. I'd never seen one up close before, only flying in twos and threes, flit-shadows in the night, me and the other girls ducking and squealing when they swooped down close to our heads because bats, you know, can get tangled in your hair and have to be cut out like wiggling wads of bubble gum. Cindy and me clutching each other in terror.

Cindy's hair was perfect bat-bait, wild and frizzy, as electrically charged as the Bride of Frankenstein's, hair with a mind of its own, the exact opposite of mine. She let me brush it for her that summer because her arm was in a cast. It was a thrill for me, dragging the brush through that frenzied hair with one hand while stroking it, trying to smooth it down with the other, feeling it bounce back up, wiry and voluminous, like something alive. I didn't know then that I'd get the same kind of thrill from her brother, when his lips were tugging on the skin of my neck, the shivers zinging up between my legs, mirroring the kinks of his hair beneath my fingertips.

The first time we went out together, Charlie took me to the dump, to look for bears. We sat in the cab of his pickup and waited. There were gulls and ravens everywhere, some perched on bulldozed heaps, some dancing on burnt-out sofas and old stoves, others circling above, twirling with rising spirals of smoke.

After a few minutes, Charlie slipped his arm around me. We sat like that for a long time, waiting for two black bears to show, for a nose to sniff the air, for a great, black, furry body to amble out from behind a wall of bust-open green garbage bags.

It seems to me now that Charlie and I were always waiting for things. For bears to come. For slag to be dumped. For me to put out for him.

While we waited for the slag to light up the embankment that night, the bat kept us company, disappearing behind us, then appearing again in exactly the same spot. Charlie took the last drag off his cigarette and flicked the butt up into the air when the bat arced over us. The bat dipped down towards it but was too smart to catch it and zagged off again out of sight. Beyond, the hill of oreless rock finally lit up, glowing orange against the pink sky. I leaned hard back into Charlie, tensed and ready for that first solid wave of heat to hit.

I wonder now if that was the moment Charlie's old man chose to put a bullet through his head.

There was whispering in the restaurant the next day even before Charlie came to get me. I guess no one wanted to say anything loud enough for me to hear, everyone knowing me and Charlie went together. But a couple of times I heard his old man's name, Hank Smiley, and people were shaking their heads a lot. I thought maybe there'd been an accident down the mine. What else could it be?

It didn't seem at first like Charlie was taking it bad. He was calm when he showed up, and he was calm when he asked Matilda if it was okay for me to leave. "They're telling me it was a car accident," he told me in the truck. "That he lost control and smashed up into a rock face." He said that part in a normal voice, but then he switched to the one he used when he imitated his old lady, when he was mocking her. "Died instantly. Didn't feel any pain," he said, like that. It was awful.

I watched him pull a smoke from his pack, not knowing what to say. He punched the lighter into its socket so hard with the side of his fist that the whole truck shook.

"It's bullshit," he said. "He didn't drive into any fucking rock face."

Charlie said he wanted to see the car. Said he wanted to see the proof.

"Are you sure, Charlie?" I asked. I didn't want to see the car. Would you?

"I'll take you back to work if you want," he said. He didn't look at me.

I said no, it was okay, I wanted to stay with him.

It was a sunny, cloudless day, a beautiful day. I wished we were going to the lake instead of driving around town, cruising all the garages, looking for the Oldsmobile.

We spotted it finally at the Maple Leaf Autobody. Charlie stepped on the gas when he saw it, made the truck squeal on the turn into the lot. Kicked-up gravel clattered and popped in the wheel wells.

He walked around the car twice, slowly, before stopping at the driver's side. I could see pretty plainly from in the truck that there was no broken glass, no cracked windshield bulging out in the shape of a skull, no crumpled metal. Not even a dent in the chrome bumper. But there was blood.

There was lots of blood. Splattered like in a horror movie.

Charlie stood for a long time, still as stone, staring in the window. I was already crying when he started beating on the car with his fists, swearing and punching. There was nothing I could do. What could I have done? I just sat there crying, watching Charlie slide in and out of focus, watching him battle it out with the car, pummelling it like it was something alive.

He didn't say anything when he got back in the truck, just put his hands on the wheel and stared straight ahead. His knuckles were bleeding. I couldn't look at him and I couldn't look at that car, so I stared at the floor. Drops of blood fell from Charlie's knuckles, the first few beading up in the dust around his feet, looking for all the world like coloured pearls fallen off a broken necklace string. When there were enough of them, they joined up together and looked like what they were. Charlie didn't move, just stared without blinking for the longest time at his old man's car. For ten minutes he didn't move, and neither did I.

Charlie spoke first.

"Rox?" he said. His voice was small and sad. "Will you go to the Iroquois with me?"

He still hadn't moved, just kept staring. It looked as if his eyes were focused on a squashed bug on the windshield, but I knew he was still looking at the car, at what his old man had done. I said okay. It just seemed like too mean a time to say no.

We went to the beer store, then turned onto the highway out of town. The road out there was dynamited right through the rock. We were getting close to the blasted rock face that everyone we knew used for spraying their names on. It was the highest, most dangerous one, and it was right after a curve in the road so you'd get a good view of all the writing suddenly, like a surprise.

Charlie had scaled it earlier that summer while I stood below, worried he would fall, and maybe even kind of thrilled that he might. It was magic then, watching him holding himself up with one arm, the motion of the other tracing our initials for everyone to see, in huge letters—C.S. & R.Q. 1972— green spray-paint floating down on me like fairy dust. But when we passed it that afternoon, our initials weren't there any more. No one's were. They'd all been painted over in big bold strokes with an ugly, cruddy brown. They didn't even try to match the pink and grey colour of the rocks. It looked terrible. It looked defaced.

There were swallows in the air over the road, flying low, swooping and swerving, day-bats looking for bugs. One disappeared right under the truck. I turned to look back, holding my breath, my stomach suddenly sick, expecting to see the flutter of loose feathers being blown in our wake, but I didn't see anything. I'd seen it once before, where the same thing happened but the swallow shot out from under again, flying whole and unharmed. But this time there was nothing. It was like it had just disappeared.

That's when Charlie told me what I'd already figured out. "The fuck shot himself," he said. "He fucking shot himself." I didn't know what to say. What could I have said?

I stayed in the truck staring at the flesh-coloured chairs outside each of the units at the motel, the metal backs shaped like scallop shells, while Charlie got us a room. I wondered if he was marrying us in the sign-in book the way they do in movies, as Mr. and Mrs. Smiley like we'd be, or as an alias like the Smiths. I'd never been to a motel before. I know I should have been nervous, but I wasn't. I was just feeling sad, staring at those chairs that were bleeding rust wherever the paint had chipped off.

In the room there were two beds, a side table for each, and a couple of lamps with identical bases but mismatched shades. One of the shades was crooked and had a dent in it. There was a vinyl upholstered armchair the same mustard colour as the bedspreads and curtains. A TV sat on the bureau. I opened the bureau drawer and inside was a Gideon Bible the way I'd heard there was supposed to be. I hoped everything else would be the way it was supposed to be, but by then I already knew it couldn't be.

We lay together on one of the beds and drank beer while we watched a Munsters rerun. Charlie finished three cans of beer in that half-hour and didn't laugh once. He rolled on his side and started kissing me. I lay flat on my back, not moving, and let him unbutton my shirt and unzip my jeans. His knuckles were crusty where the blood had dried. His hands were cold. When he got up to turn the sound down on the TV, I noticed that there was a long black hair on the bedspread that didn't belong to either of us. I moved away from it.

Losing my virginity was not what I expected. It had seemed like such a solid thing for so long, like a wall between me and Charlie, with all the arguments about me giving it up to him growing on either side like weeds. But when it was gone, it didn't seem like there had been anything really there in the first place. There wasn't even any pain. Everything seemed the same as it had always been, except that we didn't have any clothes on at all and Charlie was on top of me, doing me.

He just kept at it, like a robot. It was as if I wasn't even there, as if he was just doing some necessary chore. His breathing grew heavier and heavier until he arched up all tense as if he was in pain. His eyelids flashed open so he was staring still-eyed at the wall, staring like he did at his old man's car. Then he went completely limp, relaxed his whole weight on top of me. I could hardly breathe.

That's when he started to cry.

He lay on me like that, heavy as a dead man, sobbing like a little kid. I didn't know what to do. What do you do with a guy who's crying? I watched TV over his shoulder. Perry Mason was on but the sound was off. I watched it until the end, stroking Charlie's crinkly hair, listening to him cry, feeling the pillow beside my cheek getting damp from his tears.

When he rolled off me finally, he lay on his back staring up at the ceiling. He said he was sorry. I didn't ask for what, just looked at him lying there naked on the mussed-up sheets. Except for his left arm, tanned from driving his truck, Charlie's whole body was white. It was dark down there in the mine. Most of the men in town were like that, pasty white like soda crackers.

The hair on Charlie's crotch and chest was the same as the hair on his head, all of it springy to the touch. It was Charlie's old man who gave his kids that hair. Charlie's dead old man. For a minute, it looked to me as if Charlie was dead too. He was so still and white. I wanted to reach over and close his eyes so he wouldn't see whatever it was he was seeing any more, but I didn't.

That bat at camp was the first dead thing, other than bugs, I ever saw up close. I had always thought bats were just mice with wings, but the bat I found in the sandpit didn't look like a mouse at all. It had an upturned nose and its lips were curled back so I could see its tiny, perfectly sharp teeth. Its wings were hugging its body. Its eyes were open. I wanted to touch it more than anything, wanted to spread its wings apart the way it would have done in flight, but I was too afraid. Maybe it was just sleeping and not dead at all.

I did the next best thing and prodded it with a stick. It seemed stiff so I rolled it over. Scrabbling in the sand beneath it were two big spotted beetles. Their spots were exactly the same colour as Campbell's tomato soup when you make it with milk. Seeing them made me jump back. The bat rolled over on top of the beetles again.

When I got up the nerve to nudge the bat a second time, to get a closer look at those beetles, they were gone. I couldn't believe they'd disappeared. I let the bat roll into the hollow and waited a minute before looking again, to see if the beetles had come back, but they were really, truly gone. They'd disappeared into thin air. Can you believe that?

Charlie finally sat up and started drinking again. He guzzled the beers, one after another, crushing the empty cans in his hand and dropping them on the carpet beside the bed.

He started talking about his old man. Calling him names, calling him a dumb fuck and a coward. I thought he meant for killing himself. I sat up beside him and said something to try to calm him down, but he told me to shut up.

"You don't know anything," he said. He was kind of hunched over on the edge of the bed, like he was really tired, swaying a little bit.

"I'm gonna tell you something, Roxanne," he said. He had a mean look on his face. "That bastard broke my collarbone when I was hardly even one year old."

"He couldn't have meant it," I said.

"Don't be stupid. He did shit like that all the time. Remember Cindy's arm?"

"Yeah," I said. But that was just falling off her bike. Cindy told me.

"He did that." Charlie tilted his head back and emptied another beer.

"You're making it up," I said. He was just mad his old man offed himself. Just talking crazy.

Charlie reached over then and grabbed my wrist, hard.

"Don't fucking call me a liar," he said. "Don't ever."

He was holding my wrist so tight I couldn't move away, could only turn my face. When the back of his hand caught the side of my head I was swallowed by a noise so loud and black that I thought for a second my head had broken loose from my neck and smashed against the wall.

Charlie grabbed me by the waist. I didn't know what he was going to do. Then he pulled me to him, hugging me really hard, and started rocking us both.

"Oh, god, Rox," he said, "oh, god, I'm sorry."

I could barely hear the words through the thick ringing in my head.

Bewitched was on. I got dressed. Charlie didn't. He just kept downing beers, mumbling, slurring his words, saying how it was too late to get his old man back. His speech got more and more garbled until I couldn't tell what he was saying any more. Then he was just breathing heavily, glaring at the TV. He threw his head back suddenly and kind of howled, or wailed, I don't know what to call it. It wasn't a regular human sound, but it was loud. It scared me. That was when he threw a can of beer at the TV. The screen didn't explode like I expected it to, like I'd instantly braced myself for. Instead, Samantha's face squashed into a thin vertical line, then that line compressed itself into a tiny white dot in the centre of the screen. The dot faded slowly into black, like a star burning out a million light-years away. I turned to Charlie to see what he thought about what he'd just done, but he wasn't thinking about anything any more. He was lying back, his legs dangling limp over the edge of the bed, out cold.

I sat in the scallop-shell chair outside our door. The sun had gone down but there was still light in the sky, violet this time instead of pink. I sat there waiting for something, I didn't know what. Maybe for the throbbing ache around my ear to go away, to shrink into a tiny dot of pain that would get smaller and smaller until it disappeared completely. Or maybe for a bat to dip into sight, then swoop, flit off again. It was getting dark enough for bats to come.

The motel sign flashed on—blinking white lights racing around the edge of the big painted Iroquois head—and underneath, the neon Vacancy sign lit up in red. Way off in the distance I could see the stacks.

I saw, then, something on the ground by the truck, a small dark thing. The light was not good, but from its shape I figured out what it must be quick enough—the swallow that had disappeared on the highway. I went over and bent down to pick it up. That's when I saw it wasn't a swallow, it was a tiny bat. I picked it up anyway. Like a small bird, it was almost weightless. It felt warm in my hands. Maybe it had just then died, or maybe it was still warm from the heat of the day that hadn't yet left the parking lot.

I leaned against the tailgate of the truck and stroked the little body with my fingertip. The fur on its back was silky soft, smooth and dark. I could have cried for it, but I didn't. Instead, I spread its wings. They seemed elastic, so thin they might be see-through. Out by the stacks, I knew, the embankment would light up soon, as glowing and fiery orange as the setting sun, and when it did, I would hold the tiny bat before my eyes, hold it by its wingtips so the thin membranes would stretch apart, its lifeless body suspended in between.

Action

Erica sits in the kitchen staring at the cat, who does not have a name. She and her friend Lucy share their apartment with the cat, although he is not really theirs. He was thrown in with the lease along with a stained green carpet, a TV that doesn't work, and a smell of strawberry incense that won't go away. The man who raised the cat castrated him with a pair of scissors heated in the flame of the gas stove. Now the cat meows. A sad sound, really, Erica thinks, although sometimes she wishes him dead.

The back door to the rooftop is open, letting in hot puffs of colourless yet potent air laden with the foulness of rancid french-fry fat rising from the restaurant two floors below. The cat is sitting beside the fridge, meowing, returning Erica's stare. He has been in the same position for nearly two hours. His meowing, Erica thinks, is like a dripping tap, but she knows of no way to stop him, nor could she change a washer if the need arose. It crosses her mind that the cat is doing this on purpose; he is doing it to drive her up the wall.

It is so hot that a film of sweat seals Erica's bare thighs to the surface of her chair. She, like the cat, has not moved in a long while. In her hand she holds a jackknife which she opens and closes in time with the cat's meows: *snick, snap; snick, snap.*

In the time she has been sitting there, the sun has slowly arced around the building, finally becoming low enough to slip a slab of light through the back door, leaving it lying, like an envelope, on the kitchen floor. The increasing light has gradually whittled away at the cat's eyes until now the pupils are only vertical slits, as thin and sharp as the blade Erica holds in her hand. She snaps the knife shut as the cat's jaws come together again, wondering what she looks like in the cat's brain, whether she is elongated, or is simply a slice of the kitchen picture, like a strip cut out of a magazine.

Erica and Lucy sit on the window ledges of their respective rooms overlooking the street. Their bare legs dangle; their heels bump brick dust off the wall. They would both rather be sitting on the back roof, tanning themselves, but in the afternoons they are overpowered by the heat that radiates up from the gravel and tar, and by the rankness rising from the restaurant downstairs—the combination is stifling, almost suffocating, like being in a too-warm bath in an overheated room. It is June, and on hot sunny days in June there is never any wind.

Erica and Lucy cannot hear or see one another from where they sit. To speak, one of them must lean precariously forward while holding onto her window frame in order to see around the protruding brick wall that separates their rooms. They sit here often, sometimes making comments to each other, but mostly saying nothing at all. For hours they look down past their cooling toes, neither knowing what the other sees, watching the crowds milling by below. Most of the people they see are tourists, from Sudbury or Detroit, or families from the suburbs—it doesn't matter from where, they are all the same—posing as window-shoppers when they are really voyeurs come to ogle the hookers and the hookers' pimps, the runaways and punks, the bums. It is a main street and on Friday nights and all day Saturdays there is a noisy traffic jam, teenagers cruising in their trucks and cars, whistling and cursing, rolling stop-and-go on oversized wheels, up and then down the street again. No one ever looks up; people never notice Erica and Lucy high above their heads, staring down past their feet, their soles bared for the world to see.

It is Saturday afternoon. Erica leans forward.

"Action!" she says. She points with one hand while supporting the weight of her upper body with the other. "Spiderman!"

"Where?" says Lucy, following the invisible line being

thrown from the tip of Erica's fingernail.

A man dressed like Spiderman has leapt from a car. He dashes to a newspaper box, puts a coin in the slot, pulls out the paper, then, light-footed, returns to and disappears inside the car again. People on the street have stopped. Fathers are pointing out the man to their daughters, to small sons. Several teenaged girls are giggling, hands over their mouths, swaying in conspiracy towards their friends.

"Yes," Lucy breathes, "Spiderman."

Erica loses her job. She tells Lucy she was laid off even though she was fired. It's your attitude, her boss said. *Attitude!* Erica keeps hearing her own echo yell.

The day after, she sits on her window ledge alone, staring down at the street. Heat waves rise from the hoods and roofs of cars, mingling with their exhaust, making the street scene wobble as if it were drunk. Erica thinks she sees Danny, her lover, go into a beerhall called the Blind Goat, two blocks down. She sees him from behind. His arm is draped around a woman, his hand wedged in the back pocket of her jeans. Erica is not positive it is Danny but he has not called in several days.

Erica takes money from a man and hides it in her shoe while he undresses with his back to her. He has an ant farm and crisp hair, hard as a Hallowe'en wig. He does not turn the light off and as she lies there while he briefly grunts on top of her, murmuring at the end as if she means something to him, she watches the ants going about their business, bustling like shoppers carrying their packages to and fro.

Erica rolls a large mango back and forth on the kitchen table. It has been out of the fridge for long enough that its condensation coolly dampens her palm. Lucy, sitting at the other end of the table, thumbs through a recipe magazine. She stops at a page decorated with a photograph of a melon, the rind intricately carved as if it were ivory or jade.

"There's got to be something in here," she mumbles, running her finger down the page.

Erica sighs. "We could just eat it plain, you know."

The cat comes into the kitchen, walking silently past them. He leaps up onto the counter beside the sink and steps around a wine glass, a mug, and several plates, as carefully as if they were pools of water, until he finds a space large enough to sit down. As soon as he is seated, he begins to meow.

The mango's flat edge thumps against Erica's hand as she rolls it over the tabletop. "That cat's gonna drive me around the bend," she says.

"Yeah, yeah," says Lucy, impatient.

"I wish he was dead," Erica continues. "It would be better if he was dead." The mango rind feels oily against her palm.

Lucy keeps reading. "There's nothing here," she says, "Pineapples, avocados, coconut milk, banana leaves for christsakes. No mangoes."

Erica shrugs. "It's too hot to do anything anyway," she says. She pulls her jackknife out of her shorts pocket and cuts two slabs off the mango, one from either side of the pit. She carves a grid into the flesh of each and hands one to Lucy, who presses it inside out. Orange cubes spread apart like an exotic flower. Erica licks her knife clean, then snicks it shut.

"Where's Danny been lately?" Lucy asks. She presses her face into her half of the mango and stares at Erica over the edge of the peel.

Erica watches an orange-tinted drop slide slow as oil down Lucy's chin.

Erica goes to a hotel room with a man who has very long fingers, the nails as flat as a guitar player's. She finds he is good company. Drinking more of his Scotch than she intends, she begins to think quite kindly of him, until he tells her he wants her on top. This is not a passive enough position for Erica to cope with so she refuses, saying her knees have not been strong since a volleyball accident in school. The man, apparently, cannot tell she is lying.

Before mounting her, he admires her stockinged legs and strokes them with his long fingers. Erica cannot feel these caresses; it is happening to phantom limbs.

Erica is sitting in the kitchen listening to the cat meow while she stares at the phone. The phone, she thinks, clings to the wall like a black plastic bat. A mute plastic bat. She wills it to ring, wills Danny to call. He is never home any more.

It is so hot that Erica, sitting perfectly still, can feel the tingle of the glands in her armpits releasing tiny beads of sweat. As the beads gradually gather into drops, she imagines Danny sliding sweat-slick over the naked body of someone else, someone he has picked up in a bar, on the street, in a cigar store—she knows it doesn't matter where. One at a time, the drops of sweat under her arms break free, then trail down her sides, over her ribs, like hot tears. The waistband of her shorts becomes damp. The cat continues to meow. It is the cat's fault, she thinks, it is the cat's fault that Danny doesn't call.

Above her head, erratically circling a bare lightbulb that is not on, flies hum.

Erica receives a letter from her mother. What is wrong with Erica? her mother wants to know. Why is she so unfriendly on the phone? Why has she not come to Kingston in months, since Christmas in fact?

The letter makes Erica angry. She takes it with her to her window and climbs up on the ledge. When she is comfortable, she rips the letter in half, then those halves in half as well. She keeps tearing until she has a pile of square confetti in her hand, too thick to rip in half again. She lets the pieces loose.

Carried by a slight breeze and kept aloft by the heat rising from the street and cars, the paper flutters south. Perhaps some will reach the lake, Erica thinks. There, the cold air above the water will make them drop and they will float east, past Kingston, on their way to the sea.

Erica and Lucy are wedged inside Lucy's window frame. Erica is holding a spool of pink thread in one hand and unravelling it with the other. The end of the thread is tied to a dollar bill through a hole punched in the queen's face. The bill is heavier than the pieces of Erica's mother's letter, so its descent is almost perpendicular to the ground. When it is about nine feet off the sidewalk, someone notices it—a young man wearing safari shorts. He jumps. Erica immediately yanks the thread so that the bill jerks out of the man's reach. Erica and Lucy think the man looks bizarre from above, leaping; his head is too large and his feet splay out to the side, like a frog's. They laugh.

They play this game all afternoon. Only men jump; women notice but ignore the bill dangling above their heads. Erica and Lucy liken the men to dogs jumping for pieces of raw meat, or to fish leaping from the water to catch flies. One man hides in a doorway for so long that Erica and Lucy forget he is there and almost lose their dollar bill to him, but Erica is too quick. The man, having wasted his time, swears up at them. To Erica and Lucy it sounds almost as if his voice is coming from an elderly woman walking on the opposite side of the street. They point at the woman, and laugh loudly down at the man.

"We are gods," says Erica, elated.

"*Goddesses*," Lucy corrects.

"Goddesses, then," says Erica, feeling only slightly less like one.

Erica goes with a man to his apartment. He cannot afford a hotel room although he does not tell her this. Bodybuilding weights are arranged around the living room like furniture. As she takes the fifty dollars he offers her, Erica notices for the first time the large muscles of his arms.

Sheepishly, the man asks if she will do something "kinky". She asks what. The man, clearly embarrassed, requests that she press into his crotch with her high-heeled shoe. Erica looks down at her red shoes. They are on someone else's feet.

The cat sits just outside the back door, meowing on the roof, watching the clouds roll in. It is later in the same summer; the thunderstorms have come.

Erica and Lucy go out to watch the lightning. They each take an umbrella and climb a rickety ladder to the real roof, the one that is above the ceiling of their apartment. The approaching clouds are dark and swollen.

It has not yet begun to rain but Erica and Lucy can see vertical stripes, the colour of sharks, joining the distant clouds to the horizon. Lightning stabs at silhouettes of buildings in the west end. The air becomes completely still. Erica and Lucy can feel the day's heat in the roof rising. A lone gull passes overhead, flying a perfectly straight path north, inland from the lake. The wind comes.

"Here we go," says Lucy, excited.

The first drop falls, landing with a splat, like a bird-dropping. It leaves a black smudge spreading on the dried roof tar.

"Action," Erica says.

It becomes dark as dusk, although it is still afternoon. From the rooftop, Erica and Lucy have an excellent view. There are no tall buildings to their west, and only a couple of apartments jut up in the east. All of the skyscrapers lie to the north and south. It is almost as if they are in a river gorge, and the clouds will flow above them from west to east, following the water's course. Erica and Lucy face the approaching storm.

As the lightning nears, it becomes coloured. Some bolts are pink, some are green. Erica and Lucy count the seconds between the flashes and the claps of thunder that follow.

It begins to pour. Rain falls in sheets off their umbrellas. It splashes up from the rooftop, dirtying their shins and calves.

The water cools first the soles of their feet, then the tar they are standing on.

They look over the east edge of the roof. Down on the street, they can see people huddled in doorways, forced to stand as close to strangers as they would in elevators or rush-hour subway trains. Cars slosh by.

For several minutes there is no local lightning at all, only distant thunder rumblings and the sound of falling rain. Lucy and Erica are about to go downstairs when a brilliant bolt of blue knifes the roof of the building directly across the street from them. The instantaneous crash of thunder shakes them from their heels to the napes of their necks. Their temples tingle. They clutch one another with their free hands. Through identical slashes of blindness scored across their eyes, they stare across the street.

"What are we doing?" yells Lucy.

The building that was struck is one floor shorter than the one Erica and Lucy are standing on.

Erica laughs. She feels omnipotent. "We're holding goddamn lightning rods!" she screams.

The man is old and overweight. He is a corporate lawyer. Erica stares at the rose he bought her on the way to the hotel. She has had a lot to drink and the rose slides in and out of double imagery as the man wheezes on top of her.

Erica and Lucy are sitting in their windows. There is a loud bang. Both lean forward at once.

"What the hell was that?" they say at the same time.

"Backfire?" says Erica.

"Shot," Lucy says.

There is another bang and someone on the street screams.

Erica and Lucy look at one another. "Action!" they shout in unison.

There is another shot. The sound echoes up from all directions, ricocheting off the buildings as the bullet itself might do. "Sniper!" a voice yells up from the street. People on the sidewalk stop walking. They stand still where they are, looking for TV cameras. Another shot cracks through the distant city hum.

"*Real* action!" shouts Lucy.

"But where's it coming from?" Erica wants to know.

Someone around the corner, out of their view, is hollering, screaming obscenities at another person Erica and Lucy cannot see.

"Maybe a fight's come out of the Goat," Lucy says.

"That sounds good," says Erica.

Someone below is calling motorists idiots and telling them to stop. People are looking around as if they have lost something in the air but can't remember what it is. There is another shot and, finally, the street responds. Within seconds there is not a person visible and all the cars have stopped. The man around the corner has quieted down or been taken away. There is silence.

"Twilight Zone," Lucy whispers.

"But where is he?" Erica asks.

"Something's happening down there." Lucy points to some commotion outside the Blind Goat. They can see a police cruiser there and then another pulls up.

"Look," says Erica, pointing in an arc.

Off on the sidestreets, swarming in from all directions, are yellow blurs. Red lights flash between trees, bounce off buildings, reflect from windows up and down the streets. Erica and Lucy start counting. Twenty, forty cars. Perhaps thirty seconds have passed since the last shot. The cruisers, sirenless but squealing tires, converge at the corner where the beerhall is. Police leap from their cars. Like Spidermen, Erica thinks. They leave their cars parked askew, some in the middle of the road, some on sidewalks, the doors hanging open, light-bars still blinking red.

"But where *is* he?" Erica says again. It is important for her to know.

There is another shot. Then silence again. A long silence. Ambulances arrive.

Eventually, people begin coming out of doorways, gingerly, as if it is the end of a sudden downpour and they do not wish to be surprised again. And then later, slowly, the police close the doors of their cars, turn off the flashing lights, and weave away.

"Party's over," says Lucy.

"I wonder where he was?"

"I'm gonna find out. Coming?"

"No," says Erica. She is too obsessed with the answer to go.

A minute later, she hears the door at the bottom of the stairs close and then sees the top of Lucy's head bobbing down the street. A block south, Lucy stops two beat cops and speaks to them.

When she returns, she is visibly excited.

"We're such assholes," she says, thrilled. She points out the window to the apartment building across the street and to the south. The Blind Goat sits on the corner of the street the building is on. The building is twelve storeys high. Erica feels a cold sweat creeping out of her pores, tickling her like lice.

"On that roof," says Lucy. "A nut. A wacko. He's dead. Killed himself with that last shot when they got up there."

"We were in line?" Erica says quietly.

"Hit a guy in the arm round the corner. Blood's all over the sidewalk."

"We were in line," Erica whispers. "We were in line, but we were invisible."

Erica is alone. Lucy went out for a beer a number of hours ago. Erica knows she is in a bar somewhere still, telling strangers about the afternoon in exchange for drinks. The cat wanders into the kitchen. He sits himself down directly in front of Erica and begins to meow.

It has been dark for some time. The kitchen light is not on but the back door is open, letting in the dim illumination that spreads itself evenly over cities at night. The cat's pupils are huge and black and round. Erica stares at them. The pupils seem to pulsate with each meow that escapes the cat's mouth, as if there is some kind of direct link between his vocal cords and the light sensors of his eyes.

Erica pulls her knife from her pocket. Warming it unopened in her hand, she thinks of the sniper who may or may not have had her in his sights. She pictures herself, as in a TV show, with the hairline cross centred smack-dab between her eyes. She pictures the same image over and over again and each time it comes into focus, each time she sees herself in the sniper's sights, she makes herself disappear. The knife becomes slippery with sweat in her palm. Far away, the cat meows.

Erica is lying beneath a man who has given her seventy-five dollars. He is heavy and is not troubling to support the weight of his upper body with his arms, making it difficult for Erica to breathe. Although she had several drinks with him in the bar before coming up to his room, she cannot remember his face. She opens her eyes to remind herself what he looks like, but it is too dark to see. He is as faceless as the sniper. This frightens Erica. She tries to make herself disappear. It doesn't work.

Action! something shrieks. Her senses come alive. *Action!* they scream, *Action!*, every nerve seething suddenly with the information she has been trying to shield herself from.

Erica is lying on a bed, trapped beneath the body of a naked stranger, paralysed by the smell of her own fear. Wherever his flesh presses against her own, she can feel it, soft and sticky, like freshly kneaded dough. She feels him inside her too, rhythmically moving. In and out. *Snick, snap; snick, snap.* The blade of her knife. The meow of the cat. The hairline cross, etched between her eyes like a tattoo.

Life in the Country

I have noticed a classified ad in the community paper. It appears every week. "Highest cash prices paid for crippled, diseased, or injured cattle," it says. "Call any time. No dead stock please." So, what I want to know is: What do you do with a *dead* cow?

I am not particularly happy with this house we bought. The walls are falling apart and have cracks as long as my backbone, some even longer, bent into uncomfortable contortionist lines. I didn't notice them when we first viewed the place because Albert and his family were still here in residence. I was too intimidated by their presence, by their knick-knacks, their family portraits, their smells. Their smells are still here and I don't like them any more than I like their cows.

It snowed last night. Finally it snowed. Although the accumulation is only an inch deep, it has completely transformed the landscape. In the sun, the blue-white brilliance has brought colour back to the dead weeds in the fields, to the bark of the leafless trees in the woods. This morning, looking over the fields, I felt as if a great burden had been lifted from my shoulders, so I put on an extra pair of socks, pulled on my rubber boots, and went out.

I found the tracks crossing my path in the sugarbush. They were clumsy prints, made by an animal with a pigeon-toed gait and long fingernails, the pads of the feet textured like bubbles fossil-frozen in rock. I followed the tracks through the underbrush to the split-rail fence. The animal went under, I had to climb over.

The tracks meandered across the field to a huge dead elm on the hedgerow separating our property from the neighbour's. There were two holes in the trunk, one about ten feet from the ground, the other two feet higher. Bark had been stripped from sections of the tree. Some of the bare spots were weathered, scarred the colour of sidewalks, others were freshly skinned, leaving the underlying flesh of the tree as raw and bright as a wound. At the base of the tree, the snow was stained yellow with urine marks and there were several compressed-sawdust droppings, large, elongated pellets.

High above me an immense widowmaker hung precariously from one of the few remaining limbs, trapped crook to crook. There was a strong wind and the balanced limb swung pivoting, back and forth and around, groaning loudly as it moved.

Although I could hear nothing but the howling of the wind and the moaning of wood against wood, I felt sure there was something inside the tree.

Carl commutes to the city every day for work, so during the week I am here alone. I am supposedly writing my second cookbook, *International Beef Cuisine*, a companion volume to my first, *International Chicken Cuisine*, but I'm not making much progress. It has occurred to me that I may be too lonely to work.

One of the things I had imagined about moving to the country was that neighbouring farm women would bring steaming pies and pots of jam, fresh eggs maybe, to welcome me, but no one has come. It has been a whole month now and the only person who has driven up the lane, other than Albert, didn't want to chat, he wanted to buy cedar posts.

Albert comes every morning with the sun, to feed and water his herd. The one time I went out to the barnyard while he was there, I asked him about the awful noises his cows make in the middle of the night. Albert just smiled and told me it was nothing to worry about. "Perfectly normal," he said. I have not bothered him since.

So, from seven in the morning until six at night, I am here

alone, trapped, surrounded by unfriendly neighbours and frightening cows.

I have bought a book, a field guide to the tracks and scats of wild animals.

Every day I walk through the silent fields and into the woods, to get away from the house, to escape the cows. I find it peaceful and soothing, especially when there's no wind. When we first moved here, in mid-October, flocks of crows and blue jays passed over the land. The crows you would hear even after they'd turned into black dots in the distance. The jays were around longer, piping and shrieking, but now even they are gone. The only birds left are the chickadees. In the woods they flit from branch to branch following me, my tiny guardians.

Before the snow came, it seemed that, except for the chickadees, there was nothing at all alive out there, that everything had either migrated south or, like the fallen leaves, simply shrivelled up and died to leave room for the expansiveness of winter. But since that first snow fell, there have been tracks. A multitude of tracks. It was frightening for me at first, thinking that I was surrounded by wild animals, but I never actually see any of them and all I ever hear is the unthreatening twitters and *deedeedeedees* of the chickadees.

The variety of wildlife hiding from me on this land is astounding. In the week since I bought the book, I have identified the tracks of fox, snowshoe hare, cottontails, red squirrels, raccoons, skunks, deer, grouse, and even coyotes. But my favourite tracks are still the first I found. The porcupine's. I have gone to visit him every day. Sometimes he makes noises for me. I pull off one of my gloves and scratch my fingernails down the bark of his tree. After a moment or two I can hear him scrabbling about inside. A couple of times he has even moaned—a high-pitched, friendly sort of moan—as if he is trying to communicate with me. I talk to him now. There is no one else.

Last night, I heard the coyotes sing. Carl said it was just dogs running wild, but he is wrong. No dog, no domestic animal, could make sounds like these. I stood shivering out on the porch and closed my eyes so I could picture them in the moonlight, pushing themselves up with their front toes, their noses pointed high, yodelling and trilling exuberantly. Singing.

They answered one another from different locations. Sometimes it sounded as if they were howling on the move and I imagined their joy at meeting another of their pack. Compared to the coyotes, the cattle sound only as if they are complaining. The noises they make are so grotesque, I have no interest in what they are complaining about.

I have found some owl pellets. According to my book, they are the regurgitated, indigestible remains of their prey. I brought them home and gently pulled them apart with tweezers at the kitchen table. I now have four perfect little mouse skulls, matching jaws, and a few unbroken bones, the most delicate ribs you could imagine. I've put them in a shoe-box in my underwear drawer.

I have not bothered to tell Carl about this tracking hobby of mine, nor have I mentioned the owl pellets to him. He wouldn't understand. Even though it was Carl's idea to move here, he never goes outside. I think he's afraid. He says he wants to buy a shotgun so he can shoot marauding foxes that come too near the house. They all have rabies, he says. I don't believe him. I follow foxes all the time, track them through the snow. When they have a set destination in mind, they walk beautiful straight lines. They travel a more jagged path when they are hunting, sometimes making hairpin turns, sometimes spirals. I see where they pounce on field mice, where they sit to scratch themselves, where they trot, where they sleep. To me their tracks betray purpose, not infirmity. Tracking them is not like following a drunken man's erratic footprints on a snowy sidewalk, nor, for that matter, is it like following the cumbersome, characterless hoof prints the cows leave in the snow, always following one another zombie-like along the same paths. From the foxes' tracks I see an aura rising, a zinging, yellow aura of health and freedom and imagination. It is impossible for me to believe that the foxes are diseased.

I have taken to yelling at the cows. I call them names. I get the same pleasurable sensation from it, the same release of tension, that I get from a shoulder massage. When the cows hear me, no matter how they happen to be arranged around the barnyard, they all turn to me at once, each and every one of them staring at me with huge dull eyes. When I yell at the cows, I am the centre of their universe.

Yesterday I followed coyote tracks down the frozen river, watched various members of the party veer off, then cross paths with the others again. When they stop to greet one another, they dance and cavort in the snow. I am jealous of their social life. I have still made no friends here except for the porcupine. I think our old friends are afraid to drive out of the city in the winter. Maybe they imagine that the roads aren't ploughed up here, or that we have no heat in our house. Whatever it is, they haven't come. And Carl never wants to drive back down to the city on the weekend. Because of his job and the commuting, he is so tired every night that all we do together is watch horror movies on the video machine. I look over at him sometimes, at the reflection of the TV screen, miniature and jumping in his eyes, and think how unattractive he has become.

Last night there was a full moon. I had a dream. I was at the porcupine's tree, looking up. The sky was stormy-clouded, black and grey. The clouds raced by as if time were compressed, so that swirling vortexes were revealed to me. My porcupine was hanging upside down from the widowmaker like a sloth, gripping the branch with his long claws, swinging with the wind, his quills silver needles sparkling against the dark sky. He moaned, loud and slow and deep. It was an alien moan, not the way I've heard him moan inside his tree. After a while I realized that the sound wasn't coming from him but from the swinging limb, bare wood groaning against bare wood. The wind of the storm picked up, making the branch swing farther out each time, louder and louder, until it was so loud that I was lying awake beside Carl with my eyes open, listening to one of the cows bawling in the barnyard, the full moon lighting up the wall over our bed, showing me dancing shadow-branches from the tree outside the window. If Carl had bought the gun he's been talking about, I might have considered going outside and putting a bullet into that cow.

Pro and con letters are appearing weekly in the community paper on the subject of hunting coyotes, or brush wolves, as they're called up here. Dogs are used to flush the wolves out from the woods and onto the road, where men wait with guns. The hunters say that the wolves kill livestock, and that, besides, they have no natural enemies so someone has to keep their numbers down. They refer to them as vermin, as if they are kin to cockroaches or rats.

The other side says that the hunters drink rye whiskey and that, although a few sheep are indeed taken in the area each year, the farmers are compensated for any losses they incur. And besides, stated one writer, traditionally when a farm animal dies in the winter months, when the ground is too frozen for burial, the carcass is dragged out to the back forty so the brush wolves can clean it up.

I've been waiting to find out what you do with dead cows.

My porcupine has left me a gift! Today when I went to visit, I found eleven quills stuck in the fence post beside the tree. I carefully plucked them out and stuck them in my hat for safekeeping until I got home. They are black on one end and creamy white on the other. The dark end is delicately barbed and very sharp. I have put them in the box with the mouse remains.

I have completely given up working on my book. Not only is it impossible to test recipes when the most basic ingredients are unavailable at the local grocery store, but the cows interfere with my concentration. I don't even answer the phone any more. It would only be a wrong number, or my editor, and I don't want to talk to her. Maybe I'll start another book—*A Thousand and One Exciting Cabbage Recipes*. Ha ha. My sense of humour is coming back.

Although it's only mid-January, I can already feel the sun getting warmer. Snow falls and snow melts. It's been a good cycle this winter. The snow is never so deep that I cannot walk through it, nor has it melted away so completely that I can't find tracks to follow. The sun is becoming so warm that even on cheek-numbing days, on the south side of hills the snow melts into ice-lace that tinkles when it falls.

The cows are completely domestic. That says it all. I can think of no greater insult. Yelling at them is no longer a sufficient means of showing my contempt, so I have begun throwing rocks. Beside all the fences on the property, and around the barns, are piles of stones plucked yearly from the soil so that farm machinery won't be harmed, so that mindless cows won't trip themselves. I dig the stones up from under the snow.

I like the soft and friendly thunk a rock makes against a cow's flank. I like the way it makes a cow look more confused than usual. They don't even wince when I take aim, and just look baffled when they are hit. They are so stupid, I sometimes wonder if they deserve to live for even the brief time allotted them.

I have found fisher tracks deep in the woods, down by the river. There is always something new. It used to disappoint me that I never spotted the animals whose tracks I follow, but that was before I realized that I could see them anyway. That's what tracking's all about. Visions.

The auras emanating from the tracks are so dense now that I can see each animal going about its business as clearly as if I had been there the moment it passed. I see rabbits and hares resting in their forms under boughs hanging heavy with the weight of snow; I see a fox daintily walking the length of a fallen tree, as sure-footed as a tightrope walker, never once slipping off to the side; I see the fisher snuffling around the trunk of a tree, trying to pick up the scent of the porcupine it will knock to the ground, where, after rolling it over, it will use its claws to slit open the unprotected belly so that it can savour the viscera first.

It is the opposite with the cows. Even when they are standing in the barnyard, right in front of me, their collective aura is about as vibrant as that of a chair. Sometimes, if I stare at them long enough, I can see right through them, as if their existence is a minor mirage.

Occasionally, when I'm throwing rocks at them, I wonder what would happen if my aim were to go slightly askew, if a rock were to happen to hit one in the temple, for instance, just a little too hard, or the eye, one of those eyes that are too big. I only aim for their ribs, their flanks, their rumps, the parts from which rib roasts, round steaks, and fillets are cut. But my aim is not always what it ought to be.

Carl has gone out and bought a rifle. I can't believe it. I married a man who would buy a gun. Nothing was said about this on my wedding day. It was the stories in the paper about brush wolves killing livestock, and rabies reports, that made him do it. But Carl is a fool. Doesn't he know that accidents can happen when loaded guns are left lying about?

I keep finding new treasures for my box. More offerings. I now have, as well as the quills and mouse bones: a large cocoon I found hanging from the branch of a sumac tree, which wiggles when I warm it in my palm; a bird's nest, the shape and size of a teacup with no handle, made entirely out of tail hairs from cows; the lower jawbone of a groundhog, complete with four molars and a long yellow tooth that slides in and out of a curved cavity in the bone; and a downy soft swatch of fur that was torn from a rabbit when an owl descended upon it in the woods, wing-marks left like brushstrokes in the snow. Each of these items sends magical vibrations through me when I hold them in my hands.

The brush wolves found a fox carcass. It must have been quite an old one because there was no blood anywhere, just fox fur strewn about and layers of wolf tracks where they had battled over choice morsels or had lain in the snow to gnaw on the bones. I could see them clearly, shaking their heads violently back and forth the way dogs do with old socks, orange fur flashing like fire from their mouths. The air crackled with the energy they left behind. Gold and silver zigzags.

I found the end of the fox's tail, about six inches long and tipped with white, hanging from a spruce bough. I have put it in the box with the other things, but I keep making excuses to go to it while Carl is at work, to feel it soft against my cheek, to hold it to my nose. It stinks of wild animal, the most intense, beautiful perfume I could imagine ever smelling. It transports me as nothing has ever transported me before.

I have knocked a cow out cold! It was a fluke, really. I was aiming for its side, but it turned its head suddenly while the rock was in flight. When the rock made contact with the cow's forehead, it made a much sharper, less hollow sound than I've become accustomed to. The cow went down. Its legs just buckled. *Whoomp!* into the snow. Excitement pumped through me. I was convinced I'd killed it, could already hear the wolves singing my praise in the back forty, singing and dancing under the moonlight, but then the one huge cow eye I could see rolled in its socket. The legs flailed. The cow made a feeble attempt to rise. It lay still again for a moment, then heaved itself up. Seeing it standing again was a great disappointment to me, but at least I know now what's possible.

Carl has found my box. I have no idea what he was doing in my underwear drawer, but he came out into the living room with it. His face was a strange grey colour.

"What the hell is this?" he said, pointing at the fox tail, as if it weren't obvious. "You've brought rabies right into our goddamn house!" he yelled.

"Don't be ridiculous," I said.

"It's going to the dump," he said.

I felt an unfamiliar power flow into me. "Give me the box," I said. I know how I must have looked. I could feel it.

Carl's eyes for a moment looked like the cows', only smaller, too stupid to be afraid.

Carl has finally gone out. I wondered when he would. He took his rifle with him. To target practice, he said. I told him I hoped he'd shoot himself in the foot. Carl didn't think that was very funny and slammed the door when he left. From inside the house I watched him climb the hill, watched first his feet, then his legs and torso, and finally his hatless head disappear beyond the rise.

I stayed in the house for a long time, listening, squinting my ears to hear a shot. While I waited I decorated my hat with some of my treasures. I wove the porcupine quills through the wool, sewed on the rabbit fur, the mouse skulls and bones, and attached the fox tail so that it would dangle off the back. The whole time I worked on it, I could hear one of the cows out in the barnyard, rhythmically bawling, the sound of it riding up and down my spine like a hot demon.

When I finally went out, I wore the hat, the fur of the fox tail tickling the nape of my scarfless neck. Huge flakes of snow were falling. The bellowing cow stood in the tracks Carl's boots had left in the snow when he'd walked through the barnyard.

I went over to one of the rock piles and pushed the snow off with my hands so that I could gather a selection of stones. The first one I picked up held a sign, a fossilized spiral seashell, the surface of it as opalescent as gasoline on water. I put it in my pocket and perched myself on one of the barn-yard fences. The snow continued to fall, fluttering down through the still air as slowly as feathers from a burst pillow, kept falling until I couldn't see Carl's tracks any more at all. I let my finger trace over the fossil in my pocket, let it follow the spiral first inward, then outward. In to infinity, out to infinity. The cow continued to bawl, its mouth opening and closing with each bellow. I watched flakes of snow land on its huge tongue. They disappeared instantly.

Simple Solutions

I'm not sure how it started, or why—I don't suppose any-one really is—but in our case I wouldn't be surprised if it had something to do with my articulate angry tongue. There were other things, of course: we'd moved twice in seven months; his knee was bugging him again; money, as usual, wasn't exactly flowing freely from our ears; leftovers in yogurt containers kept growing exotic moulds in dark corners of the fridge. In other words, nothing very specific. Unless it was the mice.

It definitely began the winter the mice became our room-mates. They'd snuck in somehow, whittled a skeleton key probably, from an old chicken rib found in the alleyway, waltzed in and, with no discretion, made themselves at home. In the evenings, we'd hear them in the kitchen while the two of us sat glaring at each other in the living room, annoyed at the noise. They were very loud. We could hear them, even, over our own raised voices. He and I argued all the time. Habitually. For years.

It's probably unnecessary to say that our arguments start-ed over nothing, but they did. Just some little irritant, an invisible sliver of wood gently needling you through your sweater, a piece of gravel in your shoe. Something very small. But that was all that was needed, its very existence poking at whatever larger resentment we both harboured at the time, poking so incessantly that one or the other of us would even-tually strike out in response, abruptly and viciously, as a chained dog might do, teased beyond endurance by some idiot with a stick. It would accelerate from there, gathering momentum, me ranting, eloquently I'd think, he stumbling over his tongue, the two of us finally becoming so loud that the background clamour of the mice would be drowned out by our accusations—You this.... You that.... You—and names would fly. Ricocheting off the walls, the ceilings, like sharp-edged ping-pong balls.

As violent as all this sounds, and of course it was, it was also, for a long time, only verbal.

When he was really angry, furious, language would evade him. As words fell off my own tongue, beautifully ordered, more clearly expressing my thoughts than at any other time, I would watch his face, fascinated, watch what my words could do. Blood would first gather in the hollow below his Adam's apple, then rise from there, like coloured alcohol in a thermometer, up his neck, finally turning his whole face, his ears even, a vivid, ugly red. His features would begin to contort, twisting into themselves. It was as if all the words he couldn't release were trapped under his skin, churning and roiling there like something alive, desperate to get out. The way they eventually found, of course, was through his fist.

The mice, sensing perhaps the aggression in the air, became more imaginative in their auditory torment. They began holding soccer matches, I was sure, in the space between our ceiling and the upstairs tenants' floor.

A great number of mice, two teams at least, would gather above our heads and, using what sounded like a marble for a ball, would play a raucous game, batting it down the length of the room, back and forth for half an hour at a time. Or maybe they were doing rodent home renovations up there or, more simply, were jogging to the neighbours' Barbra Streisand collection, with steel cleats encrusting the soles of their shoes. You wouldn't believe the noise they made.

We bought traps. We managed, without incident, to agree on that. Then, having heard that mice were partial to jelly beans, we bought a pound of them to use as bait—an assortment because there *was* an argument about which flavour they'd prefer.

A little mouse was caught that first night we laid out a trap, caught by its nose, its last action, I visualized, a mad open-mouthed snatch towards a lemon-lime flavoured jelly bean. The creature was dead when I found it in the morning, rigid with a flattened snout. It must have suffocated and I felt mean. I couldn't, until later, imagine setting a trap again.

We had another argument. He started it. It had something to do, I think, with the size, or uniformity of shape, or country of origin, of the vegetables I had put in the salad, or steamed, or fried. It grew from there, each of our faults multiplying in the other's eyes, self-generating like a colony of aphids sucking vital fluids from a plant; the same as always. But then something happened, something changed. He raised his fist. For a moment I was at a loss for words, hearing only his, a threat to "drive me one", an expression I'd never heard before but one I understood. It took a moment but then I said, or more likely screamed, "You do that.... Go ahead.... Hit me.... *Drive me one.*"

I watched his face, so distorted it was unfamiliar, relax, and as it did he lowered his hand, slowly, as if it were just something his arm happened to be holding and not part of his body at all, letting it hang finally, limp as a glove, at his side.

Both of us stared at his hand then, the way we might have stared at a dinner guest had he done something uncommonly rude, stuck a finger inside the roast chicken, for instance, or hawked up some phlegm and spat it out on our dining-room floor. I could hear the mice beyond the silence we were in, the silence we had made. They were in the kitchen, rifling loudly through boxes of dried goods, cracking walnut shells with hammers, opening cans.

Before bed we set out a second trap, this time with a watermelon jelly bean balanced on the trigger, gleaming lipstick red.

The mice would often keep me awake at night. I'd lie there beside him, him sleeping, nothing resolved. Eventually, to end whatever argument we'd had, I'd have falsely admitted my imperfections, my inadequacies, my guilt. I'd have wept. And so there I'd lie afterwards, wishing him dead, the flesh surrounding my eyes, the skin of my whole face, still swollen, stinging beneath the surface from the toxins, anger-produced, that hadn't been released—going over the argument, retracing its inception, trying to decide if he really was the one in the wrong and not myself. But at those times it was impossible to fault myself instead of him. He started it; I was the victim, it was I who'd been wronged. And while I lay there, sometimes for hours, the mice would keep me awake, tap-dancing to unheard tunes or playing horseshoes on the other side of the wall.

The First Time

I remember being overwhelmingly flabbergasted the first time he actually hit me. It was a punch, a right hook that caught me just under my left lower jaw. My feet let go of the floor briefly and I flew backwards a couple of yards before my fall was broken by the edge of the counter meeting a vertebra of my lower spine. For a moment, the absolute awe I felt stifled any other reaction. Then came a brief fury, just long enough for me to spit out several awful words, and then came the pain, a toss-up between which was worse, my back or my face.

I did not weep. He did not move. For a couple of minutes we were a still photograph: a kitchen, yellowish lighting from above, black and white tiled floor, stove, table, fridge, unattractive tiles backsplashing the counter, oven mitts decorated with Christmas trees, a plate with crumbs, and a man and a woman, both expressionless, neither showing any clue as to what had just occurred. The man, for instance, could have asked the woman what was for dinner tonight, or where were his brown pants, did she know?

I forgave him.

We continued to trap mice. There seemed to be an enormous number of them. Almost every morning there would be yet another tiny corpse in the trap, a coloured jelly bean still tantalizingly displayed. I no longer felt sorry for them. They got what they deserved.

One day, I opened the kitchen utensil drawer and found neatly clipped hair strewn amongst the bottle openers, the potato masher, the spatulas, corkscrews, wooden spoons, can openers that didn't work. I was disgusted. I thought he had done this, he had cut his hair and dropped the clippings in the drawer. To infuriate me. He would do that, wouldn't he? But then I found the basting brush. It hadn't been him, it was the mice. They'd stripped off the hairs, gnawed at them where they were joined to the handle, enticed, perhaps, by traces of teriyaki or garlicky barbecue sauce clinging to the quick.

I put a trap in the drawer.

You know how hard it is to put a cork back in a wine bottle once you've opened it and let it sit around for a while? How you can't uncook a burnt roast? Well, later that night he gave me my first black eye. For what? Was it a disagreement over that spot there? Or was it a TV show? Was it the flavour of a toothpaste? Was that colour turquoise? Cobalt blue? Regardless; I was given my first black eye. I know I should have refused it, I should have said, "No thank you, those colours do not flatter me." I should have handed it back, but I didn't know how.

Possible Responses to Questions about the Origins of Black Eyes
1. Oh, this? I punched myself in the eye while I was asleep. What a jerk, eh?
2. It's some kind of weird reaction to
   a) the medication I'm taking for my sinuses
   b) this new eye makeup
   c) milk
3. Black eye? Do I have a black eye? Gosh, I hadn't noticed.

I suppose it will sound peculiar if I say that I found a certain power in making him hit me, but it's true. Yes, the incredible power of the victim. It's very simple: I'll explain. As our arguments built, it was what I *could* say as opposed to what he couldn't that made his fury accelerate. As he lost control, I proportionately gained it. And when he was finally careening with that knowledge, because he knew as well as I did that that was what was going on, that was when he'd finally grab a handful of my hair and backhand me one, or properly punch me. In the face. To shut me up.

Later, while nursing whatever bruises were rising, I'd wallow in my moral superiority: he'd hit me again, a woman. So there was the power of inflicting guilt, too. But he wasn't stupid, he knew that that was happening as well, which is why his remorse was always finally overwhelmed by his recognition of being manipulated so that, during the next fight, he'd have to use his fists again. If only to shut me up. But make no mistake, it was always me who called the punches, as it were.

But here I have to interrupt myself and say, Hey, hold on a second, sister, gimme a break. You're missing something, don't you think? Sure you had control, but only so far, only for so long. Then you lost it, then you gave it up. But that's what you wanted, isn't it? You thinking, Good, now I'm not responsible. Thinking, Good, *he's* in control. Thinking, He can hit me...hell, he can kill me, but it won't be *my* fault. Thinking, Phew, what a relief.

Except that, each time, you were not the only one who relinquished it—don't you remember? You made sure of that by pushing him as far as you did. So half the time, at the worst of times, *nobody* had control. That's what made it so crazy, that's what made it go on the way it did.

A mouse died in the utensil drawer. He was not caught by the trap, merely mortally wounded by it. I would not have thought that such a tiny animal could contain such an enormous quantity of blood. He bled all over everything, must have hurled himself back and forth in the confusion of his impending death, all around inside the drawer. Later, I remember, the dishwater suds turned a soft, baby-blanket pink.

After that I couldn't put out the traps any more. I couldn't deal with the immediacy of that kind of death. There was already enough violence in my life. So I sought alternate solutions. Someone suggested using a mixture of icing sugar, cornmeal, and plaster of Paris which you put out in bowls, strategically placed, with an offering of water beside each. The idea is that the mice will feast on this concoction, take a sip of water to quench their thirst, and then slowly starve to death after the plaster solidifies in their guts. Death by lethal constipation. This method now sounds remarkably sadistic and barbaric, but at the time I didn't care; instead of thinking of the mice as animals that can feel, that can suffer, that possibly even have souls, I thought of them simply as a pestilence, a disease that needed eradicating. One doesn't feel badly for the bacteria one kills off by the hundreds of thousands, perhaps by the million, with antibiotic bombs, and so it was, for me, with the mice.

The mixture worked. We congratulated ourselves, in a speaking moment, the first morning when we found miniature dusty footprints around the bowls, but a week or so later the smell began. Two days after our first hint of it the smell became a noxious gas; mice, it turns out, do not bury their dead. I think sometimes of future archaeologists finding the remains, perfect plaster casts of tiny digestive systems, intestines, stomachs, esophagi, alongside the black knobs from stoves, toilet flush levers, disposable razors, wads of chewed, discarded gum. I wonder what kind of worship theories they'll assign to them.

We emptied the bowls and tried to ignore the mice for a while.

How Hindsight or Time Passed Can Clarify One's Vision
I should have left him long before I did.

Things got worse. First he broke my jaw. He didn't believe it
when I told him, jeered at me as I sipped soup for a couple of
weeks, soaking bread in the broth. I will never eat bananas
again, whether they are mashed or whole. Then it was my nose. I had done something for him that I
knew he did not want to do himself. I thought it was a nice
thing for me to do, but apparently I had done it a different
way than he thought it ought to be done. So he broke my
nose. I hadn't cried in front of him in months, not since
before he'd first hit me, but that time there was an automatic
flow of tears. I remember being infuriated about that, about
the loss of control. There was also a startling amount of blood.
As I mopped it up with Kleenexes (I have one of them still,
kept as a memento. It's stiff and brown now, in a Baggie in my
bottom drawer), he told me not to be a martyr, and all I could
think of was that mouse that had died with his head resting on
the blade of a rusty egg-beater in the utensil drawer.

Fighting Back
I could tell the instant he came in the door one night, just by
the way he stomped the snow off his boots, how he favoured
his bad knee, by the way he hung up his coat, by the way fire
and steam spewed from his nostrils as he breathed, that it was
not going to be one of our quieter evenings.

For a change, I armed myself. I hid a hammer under my
favourite armchair, beneath its skirt. I turned on the TV. I sat
there. I waited.

But when the time came, when he was hurting me, I didn't
reach for the hammer even though I had the opportunity. I
mean, are you kidding? What the hell did I think I was going
to do with it? Spread his brains all over the living-room carpet? Shit, I couldn't even kill mice any more.

And every time, every single time, I'd say to him, or to myself, or to both of us: I'm leaving. That's it. First thing in the morning, I'm gone, so there. Screw you, Jack.

But the next day, there I'd be. The sky would turn Lorne's blue outside the blinds, the streetlights would fade off, the sun would rise as silently as ever, reflecting in through the living-room window from the building next door, and there I'd be, having slept on the couch again, still not ready to make the move. Telling myself he would change, really, it wouldn't happen again. And I believed myself because I couldn't believe him. So there I'd lie, in whichever position hurt the least, listening to the mice having their wake-up showers and using their exercise machines, waiting for him to get up, for him to pretend that nothing was amiss, to pretend that I had only risen early and had, in fact, cuddled next to him all night.

At seven-thirty I'd hear him finally in the bathroom, and I'd hear, too, drifting down from upstairs, mildly distorted but always recognizable, the insensitive neighbour's Barbra Streisand tunes.

Fear

I'll be honest—I was afraid. I jumped a lot. I cringed. I didn't want to be dead, not really. But even so, I'd find myself thinking things like: He'll sure feel bad if he kills me. Then he'll be sorry. He'll be *really* sorry then...won't he?

It got to the point where I felt so threatened at home that I became almost fearless outside. I was immune, invisible. I felt isolated from the danger of dioxins accumulating in my fatty tissues, from threats of war, from random attacks by madmen on subway platforms. I jaywalked recklessly. I drank water from the tap again. But at home I jumped. The smallest noise would make me jump. And there were many noises, because there were many mice.

Other Methods of Small Rodent Eradication
1. Lay out rubber snakes near their holes to frighten them away.
2. Put out unwrapped sticks of Juicy Fruit gum. Apparently they love it but cannot digest it.
3. Wait for them in the dark, armed with baseball bats.
4. Get a cat, you jerk.

There are often simple solutions which one overlooks. For instance, it is a well-known fact in some circles that cats eat mice. It had not occurred to either of us to get a cat; neither of us had ever lived with one, so I suppose we thought their reputation as pest-controllers was a typical exaggeration of cat-lovers. But then fate stepped in and a friend forced a cat upon me. It was half blind. The friend's other two cats had been harassing it, sneaking up on it and slashing purposely at its unseeing, milky eye. I had no choice but to accept it.

He was furious. "It's blind in one eye," he said. "It can't judge distances." "It can't catch mice." "What a stupid thing to do." "You idiot." So he rebroke my nose for me.

In the silence that ensued, as I searched for Kleenexes, as he flipped through a magazine pretending he was standing on a bus amongst strangers, I heard the cat, the half-blind cat who had not been in the house for more than an hour, the "visually impaired", "handicapped", "useless", "good-for-nothing" cat who "wouldn't be able to catch a mouse if the mouse was already dead". So did he. She was making strange, deep-throated, gravelly sounds in the kitchen. We both watched as, a moment later, she batted a mouse around the corner and into the living room. She tossed it in the air with a deft sweep of her paw, then swallowed it whole.

In the deeper silence then, as I held my head back to stem the flow of blood, as he said nothing, I could hear, quite clearly, the cat purring on the far side of the room.

For several days he and I did not speak. He vaguely acknowledged the cat who slithered seductively between his legs, but he wouldn't even glance at me. On the fourth day he did. He tried to disguise it but I could tell that, this time, he believed what the bruises said. I hoped he was pleased. On the fifth day he bought me some carnations. On the sixth day he made me eat them. That same trigger sprung again, by something as unmemorable as always, something as insignificant as the breath of a mouse as it stretches towards the polished surface of a jelly bean. But it *was* sprung, so he knelt on the side of my head and force-fed me the carnations. They were two different colours, I remember, pink and white.

I imagine that, seen from a distance, by an uninformed observer, it might have made an amusing scene. I say this only because I did see it, as a spectator. I watched from a distance, painlessly, from a floating position just below the ceiling. What are they doing? I asked myself. What are those silly people doing? Look at them! And then I got bored and began to look around. I looked beyond the comical struggle below and saw the cat over by the kitchen, head cocked in favour of her one good eye, ears pert, waiting patiently by a crack in the wall, waiting for the mice I could hear above my head, the noise they were making playing their anarchic game of soccer amplified by my levitating proximity.

Well, I finally left. Not the next day, or the day after that. Not until months later, but I did leave.

I took the cat. She eats only canned food now and has learned to be amused by an aluminum foil ball, but sometimes I think she must miss the mice that supplemented her diet before, and so I imagine going over there, going there on the pretext of getting her a mouse—I can put myself right in front of the door.

I have to ring the bell, of course, since I no longer have a key. I listen to the muffled buzz inside, and then I sense, more than I can hear, his feet approaching, a slight vibration perhaps. And when, finally, he opens the door, a bit of warm air wafts towards me from behind him and it smells of him, which makes me nostalgic for a moment, and weak. But then a strong whiff of something else runs interference in my nose, clovish and sweet, the strong scent of carnations, a smell that not only steels me against him, but turns me away. Let him keep the mice. They're all he's got.

Females are Green, Stupid

Ida Pike put down the pillow and swaddled the baby in a soft flannel blanket patterned with yellow bunnies. The bunnies were piloting powder-blue airplanes. The contrast between the blanket and the baby's dense black hair was not lost on Ida, but she tried not to dwell on it as she settled herself into a corner of the couch, concentrating instead on arranging the bundle so that the baby's head was balanced in the crook of her arm. With her other hand she unbuttoned her blouse and positioned her nipple above the baby's face. To encourage him to open his mouth, she gently stroked his hairy cheek with the side of her finger. The perfect lips parted and, latching on, the baby began to suckle.

Miss Pike was an anomaly in the tidy neighbourhood. Not only was she unmarried and beginning to wrinkle like someone old, but that year she hadn't staked, girdled, or otherwise bound her peonies as the other mothers on the block had done. As a result, most of her peony blossoms—pink, white, and magenta—had knelt to kiss the soil that nurtured them. That was why the girls couldn't help but tread upon them with their tiptoeing running shoes as they positioned themselves beneath the window where, stretching upwards, their thumbs cushioned on the fuzzy remnants of tent caterpillar cocoons, they could see into Miss Pike's living room.

It was the summer the girls referred to insects in the masculine. "Ooh, look at *him*," they would say, watching a daddy-long-legs struggling to escape with only one limb left, the creature pivoting in laborious circles on his fat belly, spiralling on the hot cement sidewalk. Or "Ooh, look at what's inside of *him*," in reference to an impressive variety of caterpillars, some severed, some squashed.

They swiped a magnifying glass from someone's brother's secret hiding place and used it to capture the sun, funnelling the radiant power into a blinding laser beam of heat.

"Ooh, listen to him crackle," they said.

There was one exception to this masculinizing rule—a beautiful brown praying mantis that the eight-year-olds had caught and kept in a jar in Sandra's parents' garden shed. The girls were educated in these matters, had heard about the speciality of the female, how she would instinctively devour the male, head first, whilst the two mated. Because of this habit she became their hero, their inspiration, their ultimate role model in femininity. They called her Princess Mantis and fed her flies.

With folded Richie Rich or Little Lottie comic books, they gently slapped whatever houseflies or deer flies they could find, striking them only hard enough to knock them out—dead ones didn't work—then carefully cracked open the lid of the jelly jar and dropped the insensible insects in. When the flies recovered and began buzzing about, the girls watched through the wiggly glass and waited.

It never took long. Princess Mantis, at first sitting perfectly still, would begin to almost imperceptibly sway, like a snake charmer. Then, when it was least expected, and with lightning speed, her forearms would shoot outwards and between her claws she would snatch a fly from the air. She would hold onto the struggling insect by its abdomen and pluck off first one wing with her mandibles, then the other, matter-of-factly spitting them out, letting them flutter to the base of the jar. Sometimes she would do the same with the legs.

"Ooh, look at her eat him," the girls would say.

Coincidentally, it was the same summer the boys devoted to making weapons. Not openly but secretly, in garages or forts or out in the fields. They cut blades from empty dogfood cans with tinsnips pilfered from Gerry's father's workshop.

They carved clubs from gnarled Manitoba maple limbs that fell to the ground during violent thunderstorms, and made powerful slingshots with smelly red rubber tubing stolen from Billy's mother's vanity drawer. They fashioned machine-guns out of plywood, tracing the outlines with coping saws—guns they used to hit other kids with, in a literal sense, not the Mafia one. The boys carried sharpened sticks with them almost everywhere they went.

Earlier that afternoon, the girls had been quietly hovering around the refrigerator at Kit's house after she had poured drinks into three plastic glasses silkscreened with apple slices and cherry pairs. The mothers, in the dining room, gabbed obliviously, hands snapping out cards one by one, chips clacking, their cigarette smoke shimmying past the girls on its way out the open window above the sink. The girls had been ignoring the mothers' conversation until a single, startling word was heard. Kit's index finger leapt to her green-stained Kool-Aid lips. They all three held their breath, frozen, eyes darting from one to the other, waiting to hear the word again.

"Don't be cruel," said Tony's mother, laughing.

Someone else's mother sniggered. Another coughed nervously.

The three girls moved stealthily along the length of the kitchen counter to the dining-room door. They pressed themselves against the broom closet, Sandra squatting, Donna crouched over her, Kit craning her neck above the other two because she was the tallest, a girl sandwich peeking around the doorframe like the Three Stooges from the show none of them was allowed to watch any more, not since six-year-old Diego poked his baby sister in both eyes with horizontal peace-sign fingers.

"I'll see that five, Beth, and raise you ten," said Sandra's mother, sliding chips into the centre of the table. "But I have to say, I don't feel it's fair to talk this way about Ida. Not about that, anyhoo."

Ida, the girls knew, was Miss Pike.

"What?" said Kit's mother, chesting her cards and dropping a red and a blue chip into the kitty. "Someone brings a monkey home and we're not supposed to talk about it? Don't be bizarre."

"Bizarre" had been Kit's mother's pet word for a few weeks now. Kit's father was getting sick of it. At the dinner table, he would roll his eyes for Kit's benefit whenever the word left her mother's lips, to make Kit feel as if she and he were in cahoots, which she knew they really were not.

"Too rich for me," said Billy Spozak's mother, turning her hand face down on the table. "I agree with Helen, though. What the heck's the point of losing money to your friends if you don't get some entertainment out of it?" She leaned forward in confidence, cupped a hand beside her mouth, and whispered loudly, "And you know what I'm talking...I'm talking gossip."

All the mothers curled their brightly coloured lips around their teeth and laughed loudly, all except Sandra's. She was sitting with her back to the kitchen. Over her sloped shoulder Kit could see the hand she was holding. A natural full house, kings high, but Kit didn't know what was wild, and since there was always something wild in the mothers' games, she couldn't be sure if it was a good hand or not. It would be an amazing hand if it was Kings and Little Ones. Kit's father had taught her how to play poker when she was seven.

"It's got a name, you know. Hyperhirsuteness," said Sandra's mother, sliding a pile of chips into the pot. "Raise you another ten. Besides, it could've happened to any one of us. Have you thought of that?" She picked up her drink and jangled the ice cubes against the glass before taking a sip. "Really. Any of us. It's not as if that kind of thing is predictable."

"It might just be God's way, you know," said someone "Of punishment...no husband and all."

The girls began to fidget with boredom. Donna grunted and elbowed Kit. Kit's mother glanced over.

"What in the *world* are those girls doing in the house?

Scoot!" Sweeping them out the back door like so many bits of dried-up macaroni and cheese, unwelcome things sullying her clean linoleum tiles.

They had settled in Donna's backyard under the picnic table, in its shade.

"Did you see it?" said Donna, knowing that of course they had. They had stared in shocked silence for five whole minutes, at Miss Pike and the monkey asleep in her arms, while the scent of ruined peonies climbed up their mosquito-scabbed legs and arms, that or something else making Sandra's allergy-sensitive eyes begin to run, and then her nose, until she was finally sniffing so loudly that all three knew they were in imminent danger of being caught. The window was open; they could hear Miss Pike, so she would be able to hear them. They could hear her cooing to the monkey, cooing like a little bird.

"What kind did they say it was again?" asked Sandra.

"Hibersunis," said Kit. "Something like that."

"Well, it's sure not a gorilla," said Donna. "I saw a baby one of those at the zoo. Its face was black and not so hairy, and this one's pink and *really* hairy."

"It's like the hair on my dad's back," said Sandra.

"Ew," said Kit. "Your dad's got hair on his *back?*"

"Yeah," said Sandra, "what of it?"

"Whatever kind it is," said Donna, "we won't tell anybody. Right?"

"Yeah," Kit agreed. "It's ours, our secret."

"Hey, you guys," said Donna, "watch."

The other two knelt closer to Donna as she plucked an ant off her shin. With a deft twist she separated its thorax from its abdomen.

"Ooh," said Kit and Sandra.

They were interrupted by boy-whispers, then Mark's distinctive voice.

"Grenade...launch!" he yelled.

Even though Donna's brother had failed grade three and had a shrivelled leg, he had always been the leader of the other boys, his meanness making up for his gimpiness and inability to spell. Kit had had a crush on him for a year.

A mudball skidded across the picnic table bench, leaving behind a slug trail of wet clay before it dropped to the grass. Kit, already struggling to belly out from under the table, could see the rock the mud had been packed around. Two more grenades wetly thumped the wooden tabletop, rock cores separating from mud casings and continuing off the other side, jet propelled.

The girls scrambled out and booted it for the front of the house, where they knew they could scoot under the hedge into Mrs. Benjamin's yard. From there, if they were lucky, they'd be able to circle back through three other yards to get to Sandra's, where they could take refuge in the garden shed, posthole-digger wedged under the knob to barricade the door. It had worked before. But this time they didn't even make it to the corner of the house before Donna got pegged.

She was down, kneeling, bawling, holding the back of her head with both hands. Mud oozed from between her fingers. The boys put on the brakes. The three big ones stood in a line, side by side, in front of the smaller ones. They were smirking, waiting to assess the damage. Kit and Sandra watched from the corner of the house, poised to continue their flight. Kit secretly hoped Donna was hurt bad; a true injury would stop the assault.

Mark, slapping a wad of mud in his cupped hands like a snowball, swaggered up to his sister to take a look. Donna was rocking herself, holding her head, crying and snivelling. It was starting to sound like she was a faker.

"Baby." Mark's lip curled. He shoved her shoulder with his knee.

Donna's head snapped up. Her face was contorted, her mouth stretched and ugly, snot and tears all over the place. She ripped a fistful of grass from the lawn and tried to throw it at her brother. A few blades fluttered outwards but most of them just stuck to her muddy palm.

"I'm telling," she blubbered, a threat everyone knew she would never carry out, a threat that signalled instead that she was not mortally wounded, that she would live. It was all Kit and Sandra needed. They were gone.

The dusk mosquitoes were just beginning to come out. The girls were in Sandra's backyard this time, under the flowering crab. They weren't allowed in Kit's backyard because of the blue jay nest above the back-door light. One of the birds had dive-bombed Kit's father when he was taking out the trash that morning. Then tonight, when he was walking from the garage to the house, both jays had attacked at once. Kit's mother happened to be looking out the kitchen window.

"Oh, my goodness," she said.

Kit left the silverware in a pile on the table and reached the window in time to see her father flailing at the birds with his briefcase. The two shrieking jays took turns striking at his head, beaks open, blue feathers flashing iridescent in the sun. His hat, knocked askew, hung off his ear for a moment, then tumbled to the sidewalk. Kit watched it roll a ways on its rim before settling right side up on the pavement.

Kit and her mother, faces pressed against the window leaving greasy marks on the pane, watched sideways as Kit's father fumbled, swearing, with the latch of the aluminum screen door. Panting and muttering, he stumbled into the house, his elbow and briefcase clamouring against the metal. The hair he combed sideways over his bald patch was dangling over his ear in long oily strands. He glared accusingly over the counter at Kit and her mother.

"How bizarre," Kit's mother said.

All through dinner, Kit's father kept rubbing the side of his head with his fingertips, occasionally peering at them in astonishment.

"His hat's still out there on the walk," said Kit. "Says he's going to blow away those birds...but we don't even have a gun. My dad's cracked."

"Look at *my* head," said Donna, spreading her hair apart. The mud had been washed out. "Can you see it?" she asked. "Feel it. It's big."

Sandra and Kit took turns feeling the back of Donna's skull. Maybe there was a lump, maybe there wasn't. It was hard to tell.

"Wow," they said, regardless.

"What a ratfink," said Kit.

"Yeah," said Sandra.

Kit saw a mosquito land on Donna's arm. Its body began to fill with blood.

"Don't move," she said.

The three waited until the insect became so engorged with blood that it couldn't fly off quickly, then Kit reached over and, with great delicacy, pinched off the very tip of its back end with her fingernails. He could suck Sandra's blood forever now, if they were to let him. Which they didn't.

Ida turned off the light beside her sleeping baby's crib. She drifted aimlessly from room to room. In the living room she caught a whiff of the scent she had smelled through the window earlier. Her peonies were in bloom. She had not been out of the house in days, partly because of exhaustion, partly wishing to avoid the neighbours' eyes. She knew that tongues had wagged non-stop while she was pregnant, once she had become so big that her swollen belly, the fetus riding high, was unconcealable. And she knew the talk would be more uncontrollable now. Even in the hospital she had overheard nurses whispering cruel things, and then, in the cab home, she had glanced up and caught the driver's stricken face in the rearview mirror. She was not foolish enough to believe it would or could be different with anybody else.

She wandered back to the crib to make sure the baby was still breathing. He was. Convincing herself that he wouldn't die in the next couple of minutes, she draped a cardigan over her shoulders and went outside with a flashlight, anticipating the small pleasure she would get from lighting up the multi-petalled faces of her peonies.

"Feel this," said Kit's father in the morning.

"I don't want to," said Kit, linking her hands behind her back. It was one thing for Kit to feel Donna's head, but quite another to feel her father's. He put that greasy stuff in his hair and she knew it would feel awful.

"Come on," he said, coaxing. "It won't bite."

He reached around and grabbed her left hand, pried it sharply apart from the other. Squatting, he forced her fingers through his hair.

"Quite the bump, eh?" he said proudly.

Kit wiped her fingers on her shorts, wondering why people were so calculatedly cruel.

Hatless, her father left by the front door. From the dining-room window Kit watched him hurry up the driveway towards the garage. He looked nervously into the backyard as he swung the door up. He looked afraid, like a dog who expects to be kicked—the way Kit did, she supposed, whenever she was alone and the boys appeared.

Kit's mother had given her some change to get a can of baking powder from the grocer around the corner. Donna and Sandra watched in awe as Kit purposefully asked the grocer how many bananas the money would buy.

The bananas, two big hands, were in a paper bag. Because it was an unspoken honour to carry such a gift, Kit was gracious enough to allow each of the other two to have a turn. Kit was not permitting the thought of repercussions to interfere with her belief that what she was doing was right and necessary, that it would somehow counteract all the meanness in the world.

"I hope she lets us hold it," said Sandra.

"And maybe even help feed it," said Donna.

Kit just wanted to see it up close. That would be enough.

"Do you think it's going to be able to peel them by itself?" said Donna. "Or are we going to have to help it?"

No one had the answer.

As they neared Ida Pike's walkway, Kit took possession of the bananas once again. Extending her trembling finger to ring the doorbell, she felt haloed, as if she were in the company of the Magi.

Ida looked down at the three small, upturned faces brightened by shy, eager smiles. She thought the one in the middle was called Katherine, but didn't know the names of the other two, although the pale, freckled one must be Mona Doherty's daughter. The red-rimmed eyes gave her away.

"What can I do for you ladies?" she asked brightly, hoping secretly for a sales spiel for those exceedingly sweet Girl Guide cookies she was so fond of. She could eat several right now. The maple ones. But the girls were not in uniform.

The blonde girl elbowed the one Ida thought was Katherine and snickered. Ida's stomach fluttered. She glanced over her shoulder towards the baby's room.

"Give them to her, Kit," the Doherty girl said impatiently.

The tall, rangy girl produced a paper bag from behind her back, the top tortuously twisted together instead of folded. She held up the bag.

"We brought a present for your monkey!" she blurted out, with a gap-toothed grin of pride.

Ida was suddenly under water, in an oily swamp. She stared down through the murkiness at the children's feet, at the small, grimy running shoes, one pair pink, two white, their outlines melting into the sidewalk cement. It came to her quickly then, and with great clarity—the diminutive footprints beneath her living-room window in the peony bed, illuminated by her flashlight. Flowers crushed.

Sandra had gone home for bologna sandwiches, Donna for

wieners and beans. Kit couldn't go home for lunch. She had no can of baking powder to produce. Instead, she waited in Sandra's garden shed, passing the time catching flies. She was not allowing herself to think about Miss Pike. Miss Pike was just a mean old lady, another horrible person in an unpredictably horrible world.

Kit was popping a fly into Princess Mantis's jar when she heard the door latch rattle. Her heartbeat quickened. Mark came in. He appeared to be unarmed.

"Watcha doing?" he asked, limping towards her, sliding his hand along the edge of the potting table.

"Nothing," Kit said coyly.

She wondered what his shrivelled leg looked like under his pants, wondered if it was a purple-brown colour like raisins or prunes. She had never seen it, only had it described to her by Donna, but Donna had never said what colour it was. Mark always wore jeans.

"Got a praying mantis, eh?" he said. He bent over to peer at it more closely. "We seen a female one, down by the creek, a couple of days ago."

"*This* one is female," Kit said firmly, suddenly unsure that it was.

"No it's not," Mark said disdainfully.

"Is so," said Kit. She looked at Mark's pants, at the hang of his untucked T-shirt, searching for a concealed weapon.

Mark leaned towards her. "Females are green, stupid."

He grabbed her suddenly, pinning her arms to her sides. Kit expected a blow of some kind. Pain.

"Don't you know anything?" he said. She could smell peanut butter.

He yanked her to him and did the worst thing possible. He kissed her. Kit felt his disgusting soft lips squashed hard against hers, felt his teeth. Her eyes were wide open. So were his. He pushed her roughly away.

"Kissed ya," he sneered, then spat on the dirt floor of the garden shed.

Kit leaned against the table after Mark left, staring at his beaded saliva in the dirt, hating him so hard she couldn't even cry. When she eventually looked up, she noticed a pair of rusty pruning shears hanging on a pegboard on the wall above the table.

She opened and closed the shears, feeling their spring action fighting the muscles in her hand. She imagined snipping off bits of Mark—fingers, toes, ears, his shrivelled leg. It made her feel a little better, but not enough.

With her free hand she reached into the jelly jar and grabbed the mantis. Holding it by its abdomen, she watched its arms making futile swimming movements in the air. Her stomach grumbled. She remembered the bananas. The bag was on the table, still twisted closed.

Impatiently, because she now wanted a banana, Kit returned her attention to the mantis, its praying arms rhythmically working the air, dog-paddling to nowhere. She looked intently into its alien eyes as she positioned the shears around the slender connection between its thorax and head.

"Females are green, stupid," she whispered as she slowly squeezed the handles together.

Ida was sitting at her kitchen table, staring at the tomato and sardine sandwich she had made for herself but could not eat. It was very quiet, summer noon quiet. She could hear only the distant drone of a lawnmower. The buzz of an insect. The hum of the stove clock.

Ida heard the baby make a small sound, more a squeak than a cry. She rose quickly, went to the baby's room, reached down into the crib.

"There, there, little monkey," she heard herself murmur as she gently picked him up.

Holding him close, she pressed her nose against his head and deeply inhaled.

Extremes

E very day, somewhere around four o'clock, the clouds
start rolling up like credits from the west horizon. For a
few minutes they hang over Etobicoke, silently churning
there, while above me the sun still shines. The tar on the
rooftop outside my back door is so hot that the gravel strewn
on it sinks of its own accord.

Birds become agitated, whole roosts of pigeons rising at
once so that I can hear the rush of their wings thumping the
air. They fly hither and thither, they swoop, they swerve. The
clouds move closer, expanding upwards until they shield the
sun. They move faster, advancing boldly, like predators. The
birds go silent, the breeze calms to nothing. The air pulses
with excitement, ions tango in anticipation. Ions and my
blood.

It's a summer of repetitive extremes, of slow sultry days
broken by brief but wild electrical storms. I am in love, I am
trapped in an insane, obsessive love. Every day I find myself
navigating the same mountainous terrain, up and down and
around, over and over again. I ride giddy on the highs, I gag
on the stomach-throwing lows, then race, like a winged fool,
heavenward again. It's hard on my digestion, but it is something I endure with masochistic delight. I have no choice.

In between, I coast. I slip into neutral and free-roll, steering
with my eyes closed, feeling the wind rushing past my ears,
listening to the distant rumbling of thunder, feeling the sweat
leave my pores.

Cal, the man I am stricken with, is still in love with Margot,
his wife, who has recently left him for a woman. This other
woman, Cal tells me, tries to keep his estranged wife in line
by threatening to mop the floor with her if she even considers straying back to him. He says this wryly, as if he is proud

of it. Myself, I thrive on the image, conjure it up in moments of green rage and black pain. Margot held upside down, one of her lover's hands clamped firmly around her ankles, the other on her belly, Margot's thick black hair afoam with Spic and Span, swooshing back and forth across a grimy kitchen floor.

Despite this threat, Cal and his wife see one another all the bloody time. They clandestinely meet in the afternoons when Margot's new lover is at work. Margot seems to be having trouble breaking away from her heterosexual roots.

During those sacred hours, when I am not permitted even to call, I sit at home, alone. Swaddled in self-imposed misery, I pace or bathe, or stand on the rooftop luxuriating in the storms. I let the rain pelt against me until my shirt is laminated to my breasts, let it run down my cheeks and into the corners of my mouth like the tears I refuse to shed. I dare each bolt of lightning to strike me dead.

The first time I meet her, she is on her way out and I am on my way in. It's a surprise visit on my part. Home seems just too far away. I'd never make it there. It's blocks farther, on the other side of the moon, on the far side of the sun.

Beneath my green corduroy shirt my left breast is covered with a bandage not quite large enough to conceal the bruising that is already blossoming from an incision held together by six freshly knotted sutures. In a garbage bin in a hospital not far away, absorbent items saturated with my blood have not yet had time to dry.

Margot—voluptuous is the word that comes immediately to mind—breezes down the stairs towards me. She is as self-possessed as a movie star, insanely made up, perfumed, balanced on heels that make my own feet wince. She is buxom, with the hips of someone born to pop out one fat, pink, happy baby after another. A Rubens woman to my long-faced Modigliani. My hiking boots suddenly weigh in at a hundred pounds apiece, concrete overshoes dragging me down through the depths, into the abyss. My meagre left breast pulses, alive with pain.

"Oh," she says.

I stick out my hand. I feel like a man.

"Hazel," I say. I don't know if she is aware of my existence in Cal's life.

"Oh," she says again. She looks me up and down and smiles, witheringly. I realize then that she knows who I am. I wish she would look threatened, but she does not. She takes my hand gingerly, almost disdainfully, as if I have asked her to sample a foreign, ill-smelling fruit. Her fingernails are very long, painted bronze. The polish, I notice, is chipped and imperfectly applied. Briefly, my heart soars.

Cal appears at the top of the stairs.

"Margot," he says. He has forgotten something. He sees me. "Hazel!" he says.

He bounds down the stairs. At the bottom, he grasps Margot. Before plunging his tongue deep into her mouth, he glances over her shoulder towards me. There is a look in his eyes of surprise tempered by smug irritation. It is not the look I would have wished for at this moment. We are all three close enough together in the stairwell that I can hear the wet sounds their joined mouths make. I feel myself sway, a tree in the wind.

Four days ago. I am in the bath, conducting a breast self-examination or giving myself pleasure, it no longer matters which. The sun is streaming in through the west window, warming my unsubmerged upper torso. The instant my fingers find the lump, the sun goes out, sucked behind a black bank of clouds, as if someone thinks I need that kind of chilly punctuation for such a discovery.

It is an elongated marble, firm and smooth. I play with it a lot that night. My hand sneaks up under my T-shirt. I and my fingers are in awe. Such a profound little thing.

While rain slaps at the window, I roll this lump, this bouillon cube of fear around with my fingers, tracing over and over its well-defined orbit beneath my skin. With each touch it seems to increase in size. Outside, thunder crashes around loudly, like a drunk trying to undress in the dark.

"That's a lump, all right," my doctor says, me lying on a crinkly-papered table staring at a vial of her gallstones glued to the wall. A sticker on the glass dates their removal and numbers them, sixteen stones in total, none of which looks as large as my tiny lump feels.

I am given an appointment with a specialist much too quickly. That same afternoon, in a hospital, he inserts a long needle into my breast. Blood pools into the receptacle.

"It's not a cyst," he says, dabbing me with alcohol.

A few minutes later, in his expensively furnished office, he tells me not to be so melodramatic, a remark that confuses me; it seems an entirely appropriate time to be melodramatic. I don't bother to tell him this, I merely weep.

The doctor puts down his pen. He stares at me. He purses his lips, picks up his pen again, then explains that if he believed it was serious, instead of using a local anaesthetic as he is planning, he would be putting me completely under so that he might remove "everything necessary" all at once. I think this is a feeble attempt on his part to keep me from becoming hysterical in his office. I also think that it is altogether too sunny outside. Except that there are clouds coming; it's three o'clock so there must be clouds coming. Big, fat, dark ones.

The doctor hands me a tissue from a box on his desk.

"Here," he says. "Get a hold of yourself."

As I blow my nose, I find myself wondering how many other women this man hands tissues to on a normal working day.

"Tomorrow at noon, then," he says curtly, signalling that my allotted time is up.

He smiles falsely and indicates a wastepaper basket. My soggy Kleenex lands amongst others, some twisted as if by nervous, fearful hands.

I can feel the clouds' approach now, can feel the accompanying change in air pressure, a heaviness weighing upon me, compressing me until I am the size and density of the lump in my breast.

I remember being so happy when my breasts began to sprout. The visible trappings of womanhood. I had such high hopes for them. They would be firm and round. The nipples would be pert. They would be so large that men would need both hands to cup just one, so beautiful, so perfect, that men would bury their faces in them and moan.

No such luck.

They grew too low on my chest, ripened before they had attained what I considered to be a sufficient size, and seemed to me as flabby as the muscles of an old man's arm. I'd been robbed.

I feel differently now.

They cut it out while I am awake. Local anaesthetic, as promised. I think I want to watch, but I am wrong. I turn my head away and stare at white cupboards and walls, and at distorted, wavering images of the doctor and his assistant reflecting off cold, polished steel. I can feel him stretching me, his whole huge hand inside my breast, pulling and tugging. Physically painless sensations. Neither he nor his assistant speaks throughout the procedure. This makes it impossible for me to judge the passing of time. A rivulet of blood dribbles beyond the sanctuary of my insensible breast and runs down my side, trickling over my feeling ribs, tickling me with cold wet fingers.

As the assistant helps me off the table, the doctor suggests that I should sit down for a while in the waiting room. For some reason this angers me. I say, No, I am fine. What do they think I am? An old woman? I am twenty. I am strong.

On the way out the door I see a piece of myself floating in clear liquid in a specimen jar on the counter. It seems very large. Much larger than necessary. Much larger than the lump. It is bobbing up and down. If I did not already know it was a part of me, I would feel that it was, I would know, would hear it calling to me, plaintively. Flesh of my flesh, cells from my cells, however wrong-headedly they must have multiplied. I will see it forever, bobbing in clear liquid, still alive.

I am sitting on the edge of his bed, unsteady. The room is still potent with the two of them.

"This is not a good time," he says.

I take off my shirt. He smiles when he sees the bandage. I don't ask why.

"I have to lie down for a minute," I say.

I am spinning, my breast is throbbing. I do the backstroke, swimming laboriously through the dense smell of their sex, wondering if I will drown.

I am woken by distant thunder. It makes the bed shiver minutes before it is close enough to be audible. I am cold but my left breast is hot.

"The bandage makes you look so vulnerable," he says. He seems amused.

I pull the sheet up and cover myself.

"No kidding," I say. I can't believe I have fallen for someone who could say such an idiot thing. It is the first time I have allowed myself to be even vaguely annoyed with him.

He has brought me a cup of sweet black coffee and a shot of brandy. I swallow two painkillers with the coffee, then wash their bitter taste from my mouth with the liquor. I can feel the storm coming, hurtling towards me like a bus, but outside it is still brilliant with sunshine. He is standing in front of the window, featureless, silhouetted by the brightness behind him. He could be almost anyone.

The light level is suddenly sliced in half and I can see his face again. A leaf flies by outside, then a pigeon. A moment later a massive crack of thunder rattles the windowpane. It shakes the bed violently; this is an old building. There is silence for a moment, then all I can hear is rain, on the roof, on the window, rushing under the wheels of cars. I notice then that I am lying on a wet spot in the bed.

I doze again. When I awake—the effects of the painkillers having too quickly run their course—my breast has become the hot centre of a newly discovered solar system. I stare at it. The colours of the bruising seeping out from the edges of the bandage are from a surprising pallet. Titian's, perhaps. Or Saturn's. There is pink, and blue and mauve, and an unpleasant yellow that is almost green. The colours pulse and throb.

Outside it has stopped raining, but I can still hear thunder quietly grumbling in the east. The sound is much different on the way out than on the way in, like the whistle of a train. For some reason, the sound saddens me.

He comes into the room and sits on the edge of the bed.

"You'll have to leave," he says. There is little tenderness in his voice.

I am used to this kind of thing. I have no power in this situation I have stuck myself in, absolutely none. Maybe that's why I've put myself in it.

"She's coming back," he says.

"Oh," I say, looking down at my chest. Suddenly I feel a mother's sorrow for my wounded breast, as if it is a sick child beseeching me with sad eyes and he is the father who doesn't give a damn.

"I guess I better go," I say, but I don't move. The pain is beginning to make me feel lopsided, as if one side of me weighs much more than the other. Any minute now it will pull me off the edge of the bed and onto the floor.

The force of Margot's imminent arrival helps me rise. I button my shirt with trembling fingers. He doesn't think to help me, but he does kiss me on the cheek at the door. Tiny comfort. I wait for a moment at the bottom of the stairs, wait for him to bound down after me, but his door remains closed.

Not surprisingly, I feel unstable outside. It's a good thing my feet have a natural attachment to the ground. They seem to know what they are doing. I am too poor to take a cab. The sun is out now, but low enough in the sky that it gilds the west bricks and windows of buildings. The clouded sky beyond them in the east is of the same dense colour as the darkest bruising on my breast, hidden beneath the bandage. I know because I peeked.

The air is moist and fresh and cool. I wander slowly through the university grounds towards home, shuffling like the old woman I am not. There are lots of flower beds on this route, beds cared for by garden maintenance people, by people paid to tend them, not by people who love them. I have always looked at the flowers that grow in these beds as fair game.

Everywhere, the wind and rain of the storm have folded snapdragon and gladiola and zinnia stems in two. The flower heads of the zinnias hang like brilliantly coloured mops against the dark wet soil. Guiltlessly I gather as many broken flowers as I can find, until I have a huge, multi-hued bouquet. I carry the sodden flowers home in my arms, cradled like a baby, their wetness gradually soaking through my shirt, through the bandage, cooling my wounded breast like a breeze, like a sudden lack of sun.

Worms in the Back Garden

Someone was stabbed up the street last night. The man behind the counter at the variety store told me this morning when I went for cigarettes and the paper. He pointed out the window to the place on the sidewalk across the street where it happened. He said he'd been watching TV upstairs at the time. He didn't know anything was going on until he saw the flashing red lights on his ceiling.

On my way home, I avoided that side of the street. There was probably blood all over the sidewalk, glossy and dark and unmistakable. I've seen blood often enough on sidewalks, though I've always assumed it was someone had a bloody nose and no hankie. Maybe it wasn't always that way. I caught myself sneaking a glance across the road, aimed low, but pulled my eyes back in the nick of time. At home, while I was reading the paper, it started to rain. I like it when it rains; it brings the worms up. Also, I thought, the rain would wash away the blood up the street.

I read the paper more carefully than usual, page by page, in order. I expected to find an item about last night but I didn't want to rush to it immediately; I was enjoying the anticipation of finding it, of having questions answered like: What kind of knife was used? Was it one of those jackknives that every cigar store sells? The kind that are dusty and sewn onto a piece of cardboard hanging at an angle above the pacifiers, just below the flints? Maybe it was a switchblade. But then I kept thinking of those switchblades that are really combs in disguise.

I could hear the rain pouring onto the ground around the house. My eavestroughs are full of dead leaves and twigs from the ailanthus tree, the tree of heaven. It makes more garbage than any other eight trees combined. The neighbours call it dirty. At first I was offended, but now I am inclined to agree.

Out of my bedroom window upstairs, I can see into the eaves attached to the roof of the back room. Miniature maples are trying to grow there, in the tree of heaven's trash. Like bonsai, I think. When it rains, the water overflows the edges of the eaves instead of going down the drains, cascading to the ground, which makes it sound as if it's raining much harder than it really is. As I went through the paper, it sounded as if a two-storey bathtub were overflowing beside my house. I found no mention of a stabbing in this city or anywhere else.

While I was reading the comics, the doorbell rang, which made me jump. It turned out to be a friend of mine so I let him in. He asked for a towel and a cup of coffee. His hair was wet and his muddy footprints followed his shoes across my kitchen floor. I told him that someone had been stabbed up the street last night but that it wasn't in the paper. Maybe I got the wrong paper, I said. He said that two weeks ago someone killed one of the hookers, in a back alleyway with a brick, and that wasn't in the paper either.

"How come?" I wanted to know.

My friend shrugged and asked if I had anything to eat.

"Maybe it was a domestic quarrel," I said. "Last night."

"Maybe," said my friend. He took a loaf of bread down from on top of the fridge and unwound the twist-tie.

"You know," I said, "like a man and wife, and she's just found out he's been screwing around on her." I started picturing the whole thing happening.

She's standing there in the kitchen, looking tired, stirring something tomatoey on the stove...no...chopping onions, and he finally comes home after not coming home the night before. She's all squinty from the onions, irritated already, and she says, Where you been you sonuvabitch, and he tells her, kind of matter-of-fact, and she even knows the woman, and there she is standing there all mad with a big knife already in her hand. So she calls him some more names and chases him out of the house and up the street, screaming that she's going to kill him, by god, her slippers making a slapping sound on the pavement. The husband keeps looking behind him as he's running. He can't quite believe it. He's thinking it's even kind of funny and he's got this sort of disbelieving grin on his face. But then he sees that *her* face is truly mad, wild mad, her eyes all wide and pupil, and she's gaining on him to boot. Then, all of a sudden, it springs on him that someone might be watching, someone he knows might be looking out his window right now, right this moment, might be witnessing this scene his wife has started. So *he* gets mad and stops in his tracks, ready to give her shit for making a fool out of him in public, but just as he opens his mouth to start giving her this piece of his mind, she lunges and stabs him in the gut. And there he is, his mouth already open, already neatly formed around the little grunt that escapes, the last sound he'll make, a combination of pain and disbelief, before he first drops to his knees, then topples softly forward onto his belly.

But that's all wrong, I know. It was two men. On that corner, it was two men and a smaller knife, not a kitchen knife.

It stopped raining and my friend left. After I'd cleaned the floor, I went outside. It was still overcast but very green; sun washes out green but a bright overcast day makes leaves and grass glow like neon signs. I walked up to the corner, on the opposite side of the street again from where the stabbing was supposed to have happened. Even though I was nowhere near the spot, I tried not to look at the sidewalk, but my eyes kept being pulled down as if they were attached by rubber bands to my shoes. I didn't want to look at the sidewalk but, since I couldn't stop myself, I concentrated on avoiding stepping in old men's spit. I got as far as the UFO Bar, bought an ice-cream cone—pralines and cream—and went home a different way.

I sat in the kitchen, sucking melted ice-cream out the bottom of the cone, listening to someone next door practising scales on a sax. I always seem to have neighbours with saxophones. It's a sad sound, especially when the only accompaniment is the blurred hum of traffic up the street. There weren't even any birds, maybe because it was midday, when they're quiet and out of sight, napping in secret places, or maybe they just knew what I didn't, that it was going to rain again. The sax kept playing, making me think of dirges and funerals and the sidewalk up the street.

A while later, the doorbell rang. I looked out the window and saw a strange man standing on the step. I didn't know who he was but I opened the door anyway. He said he was the gas man come to read the meter. It was the first time I ever asked for an identification card. It was a better picture of him than the ones cab drivers have stuck behind plastic on the backs of their car seats, so I let him in and showed him the basement door. While he was down there, I started thinking how easy it would be to make a fake card. He took just enough time for me to get panicky, for me to imagine him laying a trap down there somehow, prying the window open, perhaps, so he could return another time, at night, in the dark, with a knife. When he finally did come back up—probably it had only been thirty seconds—he was smiling as if he'd been up to nothing more than noting the positions of dials. He thanked me. I stood far away from him as he left.

That sidewalk up there was bothering me more and more. I could tell. I knew that sometime I was going to have to go up there and have a look, but I didn't want to go yet. So I went out to the backyard instead, to see if the worms had come up. They hadn't, but a peony had a couple of new buds on it and one of the gladiolas had broken through.

The sky was getting darker again. I couldn't tell where the sun was behind the clouds. It might have been anywhere, the light was so even. It could have been hanging on the north horizon for all I could tell. I lit a smoke and walked around the side of the house to the street and started up towards the corner. Halfway there I passed a man standing in a doorway eating hot-dog relish out of a white plastic lid with a wooden french-fry fork. Behind him on the ground was a gallon jar of the same relish, half empty. I looked away from the man. He hadn't looked at me at all.

Really, I know what it must have been. I know where I live. There are some bars in this neighbourhood that are pretty unpleasant. Places where people go and get so drunk they don't even notice that cockroaches are crawling up their legs inside their pants. Places where women can be had out back for a glass of warm, skunky draft. Often, when I'm coming home late at night, I have to walk a crooked path, as if I'm drunk myself, to avoid bumping into the people who come out of those bars.

Just two men got into a fight.

I don't know what I expected to see up at the corner on the sidewalk, but there was nothing there. There was no blood, no outline of a victim chalked in white. There was nothing there but concrete and some flattened chewing gum.

A drop of rain landed on the tip of my cigarette, sizzled it out. A boy on a bicycle sped past me. I could feel the wind he made. I kept looking at the sidewalk, watching the rain fill it in, as if it were a jigsaw puzzle being randomly fitted together, each spreading drop a piece. For a moment I thought I could see a picture forming, a moving image like on TV, but I guess it was just a reflection of the sky. It started to rain harder and then there was nothing but wet sidewalk at my feet. I went home.

At dusk I went out the back door. It had stopped raining. Leftover drops were still dripping from the trees and off the edges of the eaves. I walked softly on the porch so I could watch the worms in the garden without disturbing them. I have a lot of worms, big fat dew worms. This time they were out. Some of them were making love, head to tail and tail to head. It was almost embarrassing watching, except that they were worms. There were others too, solitary ones, stretched far out of their holes, waving their noses in the air.

It was just two men got in a fight. I was sure. Slurring words at each other in the flashing colours of neon signs. Who cares why. They are no danger to me, I thought, no more dangerous than I am to the worms.

Many more worms came out. When the ground was bruised pink and squirming with them, I jumped off the top step of the porch and landed with a thud in the grass. There were so many worms that I could hear them suck themselves back into their holes, fast as switchblades, only backwards.

Dirt-Eater

The woman next door, Mrs. Mangolay, makes faces at Saffron. She usually makes them from her front porch, where she sits for much of the day in an aluminum lawn chair, when she is not gardening. The seat of Mrs. Mangolay's chair is handwoven into white and cobalt-blue checks, the backrest a stylized blue jay. There is a chair, too, for Mr. Mangolay on the porch, the same white and blue but with a sailboat on the back instead of a bird. Other people in the neighbourhood, mostly retirees, sit just inside the doors of their open garages in chairs of the same structure as Mr. and Mrs. Mangolay's but with different designs, the various colours criss-crossing into similarly simple patterns—initials, maple leaves, seagulls, silhouettes of evergreens—images visible when the occupants rise to the call of nature or to refresh the bite or fizz of a rye and ginger ale.

In the two years Saffron has lived here, she has never seen Mr. Mangolay, or anyone else, sit in the sailboat chair. Mr. Mangolay does not come outside. Beyond his wife's gri-maces, Saffron can sometimes see the old man, when the light is right, through their living-room window, his seated form ornamentally underlined by windowsill geraniums. Motion-less, in the washed-out colour of shadow.

Saffron knows Mrs. Mangolay well enough not to take the faces she pulls the wrong way. She has decided that they're more or less an attention-getting device. Martin, Saffron's son, uses similar ploys. Martin's excuse is that he is four years old; Saffron doesn't know what Mrs. Mangolay's excuse is, but gives her the benefit of the doubt that an adequate excuse does exist. A small concession that seems warranted for a woman of such advanced age. Besides, there is always the pos-sibility that the faces are being made in response to pain.

Sometimes Saffron finds it easiest just to give a wave and a springy forced smile to the older woman, other times she wanders over for a dutiful chat, climbing the bottom porch step to eye-level herself with her neighbour, close enough that she can see the skin of the old woman's face (grizzled, she thinks, not unaware of the unkindness of the comparison, like a potato dehydrating in her cupboard under the sink. There are even several moles that could be considered the human equivalent of potato eyes. Except for the tufts of hair they sprout).

It is through these neighbourly discourses that Saffron has learned small details of the other woman's life. For instance, Mrs. Mangolay has a dead cat stuffed in the living room. The cat is called Fluffy and died five years ago of feline leukemia.

"She looks almost as if she might scamper away, don't you think?" Saffron is asked when Mrs. Mangolay brings the stiff and startled creature out into the sunlight. A wisp of marmalade fur is carried off in a breeze.

Saffron has also been told that Mr. Mangolay suffers from incontinence. This is more than Saffron wishes to know.

"Is your little one still in diapers?" Mrs. Mangolay asks.

"At night," Saffron confesses. "Still at night. Unfortunately."

She cannot imagine disposing of adult-sized diapers. Is sick to death of the child-sized ones. Sick to death of washing sheets and pyjamas. The smell of pee. Even the word pee. Sometimes she feels as if she could strangle Martin. Wills herself to keep her arms pressed to her sides.

Martin has been eating dirt lately. And lying. Well, lying about dirt-eating, anyway. He says he isn't. It is distasteful to Saffron, not only the sight of her smug young son sporting a moustache of chocolate-coloured clay, dark, wet pearls beading at the cusps of his lips, but hearing him deny any knowledge of how such dirtiness came to be. Saffron cannot, herself, imagine eating dirt by choice. Just the thought of grit between her teeth spins shivers up her spine that make her ears ring so loud she can barely see.

She hopes to god it's just dirt, and not earthworms too. Earthworms would be the icing on the cake.

At one time, Saffron felt it her duty to find a replacement father for Martin, someone to be a male influence, but she has since changed her mind. Amongst other things, eating dirt seems manly enough already. It becomes clearer to Saffron every day that Martin has an abundance of his father in him, a wealth of masculinity; he needs no reinforcement. Thus, whenever she has men friends over, it is after Martin is asleep, in that window of opportunity after the corner of his pillow has become damp with drool, but before he has woken himself by overflowing his disposables and wetting his sheets.

Saffron does not permit any of these friends to sleep over, and asks that they be quiet. Their general ineptitude at following this latter, seemingly simple request only fortifies her decision to keep Martin fatherless and, furthermore, convinces her that she needs to teach her son the simple but essential arts of whispering and stepping lightly, before it is too late. Skills to go along with, to synergize with, a working knowledge of the rudiments of housekeeping, skills she intends to instruct him in before he leaves home. How to vacuum without expecting praise. How to wash dishes without clanging the cutlery against the steel of a sink, without a clamour of plates implying possible or probable breakage, without causing or exacerbating tension. Far in the future, the bitterness of a daughter-in-law will have nothing to do with anything Saffron is responsible for.

This is not to say that Saffron is not looking for a relationship with a man, because she is. It's just that the men friends she now has are not relationship material. To be blunt, she has chosen them more to service her than anything else, to satisfy her sexual needs. She has taken them as she has found them, or rather, as they have come to her; all three arrived, for various reasons and at different times, like gifts, or free samples, on her doorstep.

Cory, who does a sensational moose impersonation after

several drinks and when properly coaxed, had flowers to deliver to Wilma Wyeth, the nurse with erratic hours who lives in the flat upstairs, who was not, at the time, home. And there's Phil. Phil fixed Saffron's clothes dryer for thirty-five dollars before pressing her against it and probing her astonished mouth with his muscular tongue. And then there's Stu, sweet, bony Stu, who first knocked on her door fundraising for a mediaeval festival, collecting money by selling rolls of duct tape, of all things. Saffron thought it a ruse until she saw his partner fumbling his way up Mrs. Mangolay's path, wearing a suit of armour clearly tailored from slabs of cardboard wrapped in the same silver tape.

Of course, the problem with these men—all nice enough guys—is, more than anything, that each of them already has a wife.

Sometimes, Mrs. Mangolay speaks of her husband's and her own inevitable and impending deaths in such a familiar way that it frightens Saffron. Saffron has not thought of her own mortality in a number of years, not since before she was pregnant with Martin, back in the old days of substance abuse, when she had the luxury of such thoughts. Now she is clean and her only stash is of condoms. She is a single mother who, because of that singularity, can never die. Motherhood has made her necessarily immortal.

"It'll be my heart, dear," says Mrs. Mangolay. "I've got the angina already. It'll take me suddenly, will snatch me of an instant. But the mister...*you* know how that will be."

Saffron doesn't, but nods just the same, while Mrs. Mangolay does the opposite—shakes her head, grimacing, making wet noises between her cheeks and her gums. Beyond her, through the window, Saffron can see the seated shape of Mr. Mangolay. She wonders briefly if he is still alive in there, or if he is only balanced in the chair in which he died months or years before, mummified, now almost odourless.

A newsprint booklet arrives in the mail outlining night courses available at the local schools—Journal Writing; Advanced Spanish; Effective Public Speaking; Volleyball. Saffron remembers reading an article in a magazine about meeting men worthy of pursuing relationships with. Some of the writer's suggestions were preposterous, but several seemed almost thoughtful, such as lingering, looking attractively confused, in the power tool aisle of a Canadian Tire store. Another, which she did not take seriously at the time, was to sign up for a mixed sport such as softball, badminton, or volleyball. Saffron, considering both her gradually thickening thirty-three-year-old thighs and her desire to meet someone with whom she can appear in public, enlists Mrs. Mangolay to watch Martin for an hour and a half once a week, and signs up for the volleyball at a nearby public school, Thursday evenings from seven o'clock till eight.

Donald is the only single male and can't be much more than a teenager. Saffron is so sure of his youth that later, when she has the opportunity, she doesn't ask his age. He is also considerably shorter than she, although able to stretch, to elongate himself, lithely. Like an otter, or a mink. He smells of sweat, but it is sweet sweat.

Except for those moments when she is actually thumping the grubby white ball over the net or teasing it in an arc to a teammate's upraised fingertips, Saffron spends each game in reverie, imagining introducing the sinewy boy to the pleasures of an older woman's flesh. She purposely places herself beside him so that during the game, as their team rotates in the undersized gym, it feels as if she is stalking him in slow motion, standing, with each change of server, in a new, invisible pool of his scent.

Other people complain about the small size of the playing area compared to the high school courts in which they originally learned the game, but Saffron likes the intimacy of it, the way it makes the game easier than she remembers, the way it keeps her close enough to Donald to whisper flattering critiques of his more impressive moves. He blushes while he sweats.

Mrs. Mangolay accuses Martin of stealing carrots from the small vegetable bed she tends in her backyard. It is only July and the carrots have not yet reached harvesting size. Saffron defends her son vigorously although, only a few minutes before, she has again wiped a crust of soil from his lips.

Suggesting that it must have been someone or something else, Mrs. Mangolay apologizes, reaches into her housedress pocket, and, working her face into a selection of distortions, offers Martin a dusty winegum. A light but bright green one, chartreuse. It is only then that Saffron sees that Mrs. Mangolay is worrying a similar candy in her own mouth.

It is not until the third week that fancy becomes actuality. Both shouting, *Mine!*, Saffron and Donald collide mid-air, hard as planets. They fall together, sweating legs and arms atangle. Saffron feels electricity despite the moisture, and cannot help being reminded of a science show she and Martin watched just yesterday, about lightning. How most who are hit and survive are wet. How the electricity follows the conduction route most appealing, a sheathing of rainwater. How these people are found not only unconscious but naked, their garments blown away from their bodies. How those clothes, she imagines now, lie strewn haphazardly about them, shirts and skirts and pants flung aside as if by first-time lovers, careless and in a hurry.

Mrs. Mangolay is watching Friends when Saffron and Donald come in. "Help yourself," she says, indicating a bowl of microwave popcorn on the coffee table, as if it is hers to offer. Saffron, in return, politely offers Mrs. Mangolay the final ten minutes of the show, but, happily, the babysitter declines, the episode being a rerun.

From the other side of the screen door, after taking the money owed her, Mrs. Mangolay tells Saffron that, oh, by the way, she had to give Martin a little spanking.

Alarmed, Saffron asks, "For what?"

Mrs. Mangolay sways forward and whispers sideways into the screen, "He was naughty." The phrase comes with wet sucking sounds, facial contortions, and the sweet bouquet of alcohol-free port wine.

"Naughty?" says Saffron. Barely containing herself. She has never spanked Martin, never slapped him, never smacked him, never even yanked him by his tiny upper arm. "What did he do?"

"You know. Boys will be boys. Not to worry." Mrs. Mangolay slides away down the steps. "Good night then, love," she calls back to Saffron.

Before she can respond, Donald is upon her.

There follow two weeks of bliss, or the closest to bliss that Saffron has ever experienced, and not just sexually, for she falls for Donald. It turns out that he is smart and funny and he wipes down the shower stall when he is done. He writes impromptu love poems to her, tracing the letters out large with his fingertip on her naked back. He whispers, not only sweet nothings in her ear, but simply to be quiet.

Smitten, Saffron, after only a week and a half of nighttime trysts, allows him to visit on a Saturday afternoon, introduces him to her son. In the backyard, while she lounges on a partially crippled chaise, sipping a hard lemonade, Saffron watches as Donald grasps Martin by his right wrist and ankle, watches him airplane her boy around and around until the child has shrieked himself breathless and the two lie panting and giggling in the grass.

Saffron receives a phone call from a woman who identifies herself as Donald's mother. Before she can thank the woman for raising her son so well, she is lit into.

"You're sick," the woman says. "Sick. What's wrong with

145

you? I should have you charged."

"What are you talking about?" Saffron asks.

"For godsake," the woman says, "he just turned sixteen. Six*teen*!"

Saffron puts it together quickly, standing in the kitchen, still holding the now silent telephone receiver. The smooth chest, the beatnik-like sparseness and softness of facial hair, the slavish attentiveness. How his "going back to school" would be high school, not college or university. Why, when she asked what he was studying, he had not answered evasively, as she had thought, but honestly. *Some of everything.* Why his summer job was so menial.

Although she is not the type, Saffron considers banging either the phone receiver or her head against the wall.

Oh lord, she thinks, his bones are probably still soft, the plates of his skull not yet fused together.

Saffron knows she won't be able to look at Donald again, knows there will be no more volleyball, no more anything. Already it feels like incest. As if she has been making love to a long-lost son, one given up at birth and, after years of searching, found. She's old enough.

Later, bathing Martin, she feels queasy, almost sick to her stomach. She can see him, her son, in twelve years, his miniature penis grown man-sized, Donald-sized. In real life she also sees an odd mark on his back, a deep-coloured bruise; when quizzed about how it came to be, he cannot seem to recall.

The next morning Saffron is mixing the dry ingredients of a puddingcake mix with the wet ones called for on the box when Martin comes in, face filthy, dirt lipsticking his mouth, jaws working, chewing.

"Come here," she says.

She works her fingers between his mini-toothed jaws, hooks something hard and irregular-shaped amongst gravel-feeling bits, draws this larger object out with a curled, saliva-slick forefinger. A chunk of strong-smelling carrot, so freshly torn from the earth that it might still be alive.

"You little rat," Saffron says, and drags Martin by his arm roughly, hauls him across the kitchen, his legs dancing to keep up, out the back door. She sees Mrs. Mangolay immediately, down the rise, beyond the fringe of hedge that serves only as a symbolic separation of their backyards. The old woman is at the far end of her property, shadows of hanging laundry fluttering over her. She is sprawled out, lying on her back in her vegetable bed, a straw broom incongruously beside her.

Saffron hoists Martin into her arms and hurdles over the straggly hedge. At the garden, she drops to her knees and releases the boy. Mrs. Mangolay appears not to be breathing. Her eyes are closed. Saffron presses her ear against the woman's bosom, hears nothing, but smells the resinous odour of crushed tomato leaves.

"Don't move," she says to Martin as she springs to her feet and runs up the slope to the Mangolays' house.

The back door is locked. She runs around to the front, calling to Mr. Mangolay. Up the steps, past the woven chairs, through the door.

The smell slugs her, hits her like a wall of acrid smoke, the rank and gassy stench of human excrement and urine. Most of it not fresh. She gags, clutches her throat, instinctively hunches over, squatting, seeking fresher air down low, as if there is a fire. In the dimness of the living room, Mr. Mangolay is sitting before her, in a plaid easy chair, facing the window. His mouth is slack, his stubbly chin glimmering with drool, both liquid and dried. His eyes are open, but are reacting no more to Saffron's presence than to anything else.

Her own eyes stinging, Saffron searches for the phone, finds it on an end table beside Fluffy, the taxidermied cat.

It is only while she is giving the address to the 911 operator that she sees that Mr. Mangolay is strapped to his chair, two worn leather belts, a brown one and a black one, buckled together around his chest. He probably could not sit upright without their help. Saffron thinks how very sad that is, how very sad all of this is, while being asked if she is trained in CPR. She isn't. AR? She thinks she remembers from Red Cross swimming lessons, years ago. Try that then, she is told, until the medics arrive. And keep the victim warm. Saffron has not thought of Mrs. Mangolay as a victim until the 911 operator suggests it.

She grabs a crocheted afghan off a couch and runs outside again, sees Martin when she rounds the back corner of the house. He is squatting beside Mrs. Mangolay, his little hand fishing in the fallen woman's dress pocket. Saffron screams his name. Martin looks up, stuffing another winegum into his already chipmunked cheeks.

In long, running strides, Saffron is upon him. She drops the afghan, grabs the boy by his T-shirt collar, yanks him up, squeezes his cheeks in her hand, distorting his face, forcing his mouth to open like a carp's.

"Spit them out!" she hisses, him squirming, struggling.

When she sees his lips purse together tight in defiance, she slaps him. The little ghoul. Robbing the dead. Full force, hard.

This confrontation takes five seconds, ten seconds max, but long seconds during which Saffron could have been starting, ought to have been starting, artificial respiration. Even if it is already too late.

She is kneeling over Mrs. Mangolay, hauling from her memory long-ago-learned details, first hooking her finger the same way inside the motionless old woman's mouth as she did inside her son's not minutes before, searching, supposedly, for seaweed or other debris, or candy, feeling the upper teeth, the pallet, the lower teeth not there, just hard, moist gums. She gropes farther back, probing for the missing plate, feeling the soft wet tongue, the spongy entrance to the throat. Finding nothing, she tilts the head back, straightening the neck, the trachea, pinching the nostrils closed, smelling sweet fruitiness before clamping mouth to mouth, feeling the wrinkles of Mrs. Mangolay's lips but also a surprising softness. Feeling, too, the tickle of the woman's wispy moustache. Saffron thinks then, unforgivably, of Donald's delicate, pubescent excuse for one. How could she be so stupid? So blind? These thoughts turn the first air she blows into Mrs. Mangolay's lungs into a deep sigh of defeat. Then she is just blowing in and counting, blowing and counting.

Beyond the hollow silence created by this emergency, this focus on rhythmic breathing and counting, Saffron slowly becomes aware of a wailing sound. The siren, she first assumes, of the fast-approaching emergency vehicle, the ambulance. But the sound does not get louder. On the contrary, it is becoming more distant, softer, fading away, it seems. Saffron fights a panicky need to break the tempo so she can scream, Come back! Come back! But she won't allow herself to, then understands she needn't, because the paling wail has been compressed into a high-pitched yet quiet and familiar whine. She is hearing Martin, who is somewhere behind her, where she cannot see, out of range—Martin, whom she has struck, for the first time, with her own hand. This is instantly so unbearable to her, the fact of it, not being able to address it, to touch him, to hold him, being trapped, latched by some sense of civil duty, some ridiculous sense of humanity, to this dead woman's mouth, that Saffron can only will herself to fall back into the rhythm of the breathing, the counting, so that she cannot hear her son, now alternately hiccupping and whimpering, forcing herself to succumb to the soothing repetition until all she can feel are the shadows of the laundry fluttering across the back of her neck and her bare arms, butterfly kisses from a boy not yet old enough to know better.